MW00910117

This special signed edition
is limited to **750**
        numbered copies and **26** lettered copies.

This is copy _126_ .

COLONEL
RUTHERFORD'S
COLT

COLONEL RUTHERFORD'S COLT

Lucius Shepard

Subterranean Press · 2003

Colonel Rutherford's Colt
Copyright © 2002 by Lucius Shepard
All rights reserved.

Dust jacket illustration
Copyright © 2003 by J. K. Potter
All rights reserved.

Interior design
Copyright © 2003 by Tim Holt. All rights reserved.

ISBN
1-931081-74-3

Subterranean Press
P. O. Box 190106
Burton, MI 48519

e-mail:
subpress@earthlink.net

website:
www.subterraneanpress.com

Rita Whitelaw and Jimmie Roy Guy seemed like a strange couple to everyone but themselves. No one could understand how this boyish man of twenty-nine had come to partner with a flinty Blackfoot woman ten, eleven years older and looking every day of it…though even her harshest detractors would not deny that Rita was of a type certain men found alluring. She stood nearly six feet tall — taller yet in her fancy boots — and usually wore a hawk feather woven into her braid, and her finely sculpted features brought to mind a long-dead movie actress whose name folks could never quite recall. But there was something off-putting about her, something not-beautiful. Too much crazy luck and reckless living in her eyes. She gave the impression you might strike sparks from that hard-held mouth if you brushed her lips with a kiss. By contrast, Jimmy was towheaded, several inches shorter, with an amiable hillbilly face and grayish blue eyes whose steadiness supported the air of distracted calm with which he met the world. Some would tell you that he wasn't right in the head, and Rita was taking advantage of him. Then there were those who argued that the situation was exactly the opposite. Whatever their opinion, when people saw Rita and Jimmy sitting behind their tables at the gun shows, they found no reasonable way of fitting them together, no evidence of love or any ordinary mutuality. The only thing they appeared to have in common was each other.

Thursday, the opening morning of the Issaquah Gun Show, began as did many of their mornings in a campsite just off the expressway, this one a twenty-minute drive west of the Cascades in Washington State. A heavy mist ghost-dressed the landscape, lending the bunkerlike building that housed the bathrooms a mysterious presence and making shadowy menaces of the sickly spruce that sentried it. The rush of high-speed traffic sounded like reality had sprung a serious leak. Rita had thrown on a plaid wool jacket over a denim shirt and leather pants, and was stuffing sleeping bags into the rear of a brown Dodge van with GUY GUNS lettered in black and yellow on the side. Jimmy, wearing jeans and a tan suede sport coat that had seen better days, was standing off a ways, his head tipped back as if contemplating a judgment on the weather.

"Believe we got one coming today," he said. "One with some move on it."

"You always say the same thing," Rita said curtly. "About half the time you wrong."

"I can feel them out there," he said. "They all trying to come our way, just sometimes they don't make it to the table."

She slammed shut the rear door of the van. "Yeah…we'll see."

They drove the slow lane for nine miles to the Issaquah exit and turned off the access road into a strip mall. Rain began to slant against the windshield. There were deep puddles everywhere. The blacktop was a regulated river running straight between one-story banks of burger taco pizza, with big shiny metal fish passing along it two-by-two. They ate a McDonald's breakfast in the van, staring out at a tire dealership bulking up beyond a row of dumpsters—a huge tire with a white clown face bulging from its middle was stuck on a pole atop the roof. Jimmy had gone for the sausage, egg and cheese biscuit. Rita was working on a Quarter Pounder and fries supersized.

"How you eat hamburger damn near every morning of your life, I'll never know," Jimmy said, and had a bite of biscuit. "That ain't no real breakfast."

Rita said something with her mouth full and he asked her to repeat it.

"I said —" she swallowed, wiped her mouth with a napkin " —you're eating lard." She took a swig of Diet Coke. "That thing you're eating, meat's about half lard. Biscuit, too."

"Least it tastes like breakfast."

Rita let out with a give-me-strength sigh, like she knew she was dealing with a child. They continued eating, and into Jimmy's mind, which generally ran along unimaginative lines, came the image of a sapling palm bathed in golden early morning sun. As the image hung there, superimposed over the customary traffic of his thoughts, it began to acquire detail. Dew beaded its dark green fronds. Glowing dust motes quivered in shafts of light like excited atoms. A speckled lizard clung to the trunk. When it faded he said, "Now I know we got one coming! It's talking at me already."

Rita popped a fry into her mouth, chewed. "What's it say?"

He told her about the palm tree.

She was studying the fine print on the back of a candy bar wrapper she was preparing to tear open. "Sounds like a real pretty story."

"I know it ain't talking at me," he said, annoyed by her indifference. "It's a figure of speech is all. I ain't as simple as you think."

"You don't know what I think," she said flatly, and peeled back the wrapper; she had a bite of the candy bar.

"What the hell you see in me?" he asked. "It can't be much. You treat me like a damn idiot about half the time."

The rain picked up, filming across the windshield, washing the tire dealership into a blur of blue and white.

"How I treat you the rest of the time?" Rita asked.

"You treat me nice," he said sullenly. "But that don't..."

"Well, maybe you oughta consider that before you snap at me. Maybe you oughta assume when I don't treat you nice, I got things on my mind."

That worried him. "What...? Something bothering you?"

"Something's always bothering me, Jimmy." She stuffed the empty fry carton into the McDonald's bag, balled it up, rolled down the window and heaved the bag in the direction of a dumpster. Rain slashed at her shoulder as she wrangled the window closed. "I'm thinking about bills. If it ain't bills, it's about getting the van looked at. About whether we should do the show in North Bend. About all the shit you don't have to handle."

"I can do my share, you just let me."

"Oh, yeah! I seen you do your share. Last time I left you to handle things, we had collection people calling every five minutes. You want to know what I see in you?" Her black eyes nailed him so hard, he felt stricken. "I tell you that, chances are I won't see it no more."

She turned the ignition key, gunned the engine. "Finish your breakfast. Y'know they won't have nothing good at the show."

He was remembering the palm tree, wondering where it grew, Mexico or Brazil...maybe Cuba. It took him a few seconds to respond.

"I ain't eating no damn lard," he said.

Tucked into a corner of the Issaquah armory, away from the central pathology of the gun show, where beneath ceiling-long trays of fluorescent light, teenagers with tipped hair, relief-map acne, and Satanist T-shirts fondled assault rifles, and wary militia types with graying prophet's beards passed out tracts to Kiwanis Club members and fat men with trucker wallets, and novelty dealers sold Buck Owens switchblades and WWII bomb casings, and families shopped at the fancy

booths for a nice pearl-handled carry-along with decent stopping power for Mom…far from all that, tucked into a rear
corner of the building, were the two tables assigned to Guy
Guns. Unlike the other dealers, Jimmy and Rita suspended
no banner behind their tables. They appealed to a select cli-
entele, and the people with whom they did business knew
how to find them. In their display cases a .42 caliber Smith
and Wesson revolver that had once belonged to Teddy
Roosevelt, a .38 caliber Beretta with a golden grip presented
to Elliot Ness by the Chicago Chamber of Commerce, and a
single-shot derringer wielded by the Civil War spy Belle Star
nested in among weapons of less noble yet no less authentic
pedigree, some dull and evil-looking amid folds of purple
velvet, others with fancy plating and inlays appearing harm-
less as jewelry. Most people who wandered back into their
corner would glance at the price tags and skate away. Occasionally a man wearing a T-shirt bearing a brave slogan such
as If You Want My Gun You Can Pry It From My Cold Dead
Hand would linger over the cases and ask a question or two
before moving on. And once a group of Russian men who
had been buying switchblades in volume debated whether
or not to make an offer on the Ness Beretta.

"Is Elliot Ness the Untouchable guy, yes?" their spokes-
man asked, and when Jimmy said yeah, it was indeed that
Elliot Ness, and showed him the certificate of authenticity,
the Russians huddled up. After a brief discussion, the spokes-
man — a burly, affable sort with a watermelon gut and his
head shaved to stubble — came back with an offer that was
about two-thirds the asking price.

"This gun's got a lot of move," Jimmy told him. "It's
bound to move before end of business tomorrow." He
dangled the price tag in front of the bewildered Russian's
face. "But it ain't moving for a dollar less than it says right
here."

"We coulda used that sale," Rita said as they stood watching the Russians push into the crowded center aisle.

"He'll be back before closing." Jimmy lifted the top of the display case and gently placed the Beretta next to a delicate fowling piece embellished with mother-of-pearl — male and female together. "Come Saturday night he'll be hauling it out at a party, telling everybody he's—" he did a mud-thick Russian accent " — the Untouchable guy."

"Your call," said Rita and went back to her magazine.

One o'clock came, and Jimmy's stomach started growling. All the food concession had to offer were corn dogs and warmed-over fries and rotisserie-grilled Polish sausages that resembled blistered rubber tubes. He was debating these choices when a woman in a blue flowered dress approached the table. Smoky hair bobbed at the shoulders and a fair complexion. Peaches and cream, his daddy would have said. A little plump, but pretty in a TV-housewife way. She would have looked a lot prettier, he thought, if she'd been less worried. Her mouth was screwed up tight, her brow furrowed. Dark pouches beneath her eyes suggested that she hadn't been getting much sleep. She had tried to fix herself up with powder and bright cherry lipstick, but this had not disguised the effects of whatever was troubling her. He guessed she was about Rita's age, though it would have been a neat trick to find a pair of women more opposite. Where Rita was all lean angles and cheekbone sharpness and aggression, this woman was diminutive and gave the impression of vulnerability and soft curves everywhere. She kept an arm wrapped about a large brown purse, as if afraid what was inside would squirm out should she let go.

"Are you Mister Guy?" In its gentle probing, the woman's sugary voice reminded Jimmy of his third grade teacher asking if she could see what he was writing in his notebook. He said yeah, he sure was. She offered her hand and said, "My name is Loretta Snow," almost making it into a question. She had a quick look behind her. "I'm told you buy guns?"

"We buy historical weapons," Jimmy said. "Y'know… guns belonged to famous people, or else they were used in some famous battle. Or a crime."

"I might just have one for you, then." She opened the purse and removed something covered in a gray cloth. The instant she began to unwrap it, Jimmy knew she had brought him the palm-tree gun, and when she handed it over, a Colt .45 Model 1911 with a well-oiled gray finish, he could feel a tropical heat in his head, and felt also the shape of a story. Blood and passion, hatred and love.

Rita leaned in over his shoulder, and he held it up for her to see. "Original model. No crescent cuts back of the trigger." She made a noncommittal noise.

"It used to belong to Bob Champion," Ms. Snow said. "He might not be famous enough for you, but people know him around here."

Jimmy didn't recognize the name, but Rita said, "You mean the white-power guy?"

Ms. Snow seemed surprised that she had spoken. She folded the cloth and said quietly, "That'd be him. I was his wife for eight years."

Rita scoured her with a stare. To Jimmy she said, "Champion's the one robbed them armored trucks over in Idaho. Son of a bitch is a star-spangled hero to every racist fuck in America."

Ms. Snow took the hit fairly well, but when two prepubescent boys juked past behind her, laughing, jabbing and slashing at each other with sheathed knives, she gave a start and looked shaken.

"You sell this privately, you'll get more'n I can pay," Jimmy told her, ignoring Rita, who was making angry speech with her eyes. "I can move it for you, but we get forty percent markup."

"I know." Ms. Snow stuffed the cloth back into her purse. "I had a man offer me four thousand, but I wouldn't let him have it."

"Four thousand's high," Jimmy said. "I'd do 'er, I was you."

"No sir," she said. "I won't sell to him. In fact, I don't want you to sell to him, neither. That'd be a condition of me selling it to you."

Rita started to object, but Jimmy jumped in first. "How come you won't sell to him?"

"I believe I'll let that stay my business," said Ms. Snow.

Rita snatched the gun from Jimmy and held it out to Ms. Snow. "Then you can let this here stay your business, too."

After a moment's indecision Ms. Snow said, "The man's name is Raymond Borchard. He calls himself Major, but I don't know if he was a real soldier. He's got a place up in the mountains where he marches around with some other fools and shoots at targets and talks big about challenging the government. He venerates Bob. They all do. He told me Bob's gun was a symbol. If they had it to look at, he said it'd make them stronger for what was to come."

"I can't understand why you got a problem with that," said Rita. "Seeing how you in the same damn club."

Ms. Snow met Rita's contempt with cool reserve. "You don't know me, ma'am."

This tickled Jimmy — Rita hated to be called ma'am. She set the gun down on the table and said to Ms. Snow, "I don't wanna know ya...*ma'am*."

"I was barely eighteen when I married Bob Champion," Ms. Snow went on in a defiant tone. "Far as I could tell, he was a good man. Hard-working and devout. Something went wrong with him. Maybe it was the money trouble...I still don't understand it. It just seemed like one minute he was Bob, and the next he was somebody else. I was twenty-three and I had three babies. Maybe I should have left him. But I simply did not know where to go." A quaver crept into her voice. "If you want to damn me for that, go ahead. I don't care. I've got a good job's been offered me in Seattle, and all I care about is getting enough money to move me and my kids away from here...and away from Ray Borchard."

Rita gave Jimmy a you-deal-with-this-shit look and had a seat at their second table. Jimmy picked up the Colt and settled the grip in his palm. He felt the weight of the story accumulating inside his head. "Tell you what," he said to Ms. Snow. "I'll take the gun on consignment this weekend and the next. For the show they got over in North Bend. If I move it before I leave North Bend, I'll cut myself twenty percent commission. If it don't move, I'll make you an offer and you can do what you want."

"I suppose that's reasonable," Ms. Snow said hesitantly.

"It's a helluva lot more than reasonable!" Rita scraped back her chair and came over. "We don't take nothing on consignment."

"We can do this one," said Jimmy calmly. "We got enough we can help someone out once in a while."

"Jimmy!"

"We going to move the goddamn Beretta, Rita!" He fished out a handful of twenties from the cash box. "Here. You go on ahead and celebrate. And get us a room at the Red Roof."

He thought he could feel the black iron of her stare branding a two-eyed shape onto the front of his brain. She grabbed the bills and stuffed them in her shirt pocket. "I'll leave you a key at the desk," she said. "I'll be at Brandywines." She expressed him another heated look. "You better sell the damn Beretta." Then she stalked off, shoving aside a portly balding man wearing a camo field jacket and pants.

"I didn't mean to cause trouble," Ms. Snow said, but Jimmy gave a nonchalant wave and said, "That's just me and Rita. We got what you call a volatile relationship."

"Oh." Volatile relationships did not appear to be within the scope of Ms. Snow's experience.

Jimmy began writing a receipt. "You better tell me what this Borchard fella looks like 'case he tries to pass himself off as someone else."

"That's not his style. He'll come right out with who he is. He expects everyone'll be impressed."

"Yeah, but…" Jimmy stopped writing. "Supposing he sends one of his men to buy it? Whyn't you hang around, and I'll buy you a cup of coffee? You can tell me if you spot someone familiar."

Ms. Snow faded back from the table, clutching the purse to her stomach. "No sir," she said. "I won't deal with those people. That's why I gave you the gun. So I won't have to."

"All right." Jimmy finished with the receipt. "But I'm going to need your information. That way I can check with you when I get a buyer." He handed her a business card and she scribbled down a number and an address.

Ms. Snow pivoted out from the table, smooth as a dance turn, then stopped and glanced back, affording Jimmy a view of a sleek flank sheathed in flimsy, flowered blue. "I should be home most of the weekend if you need to give me a call," she said, and smiled her cherry smile. "Thank you so much…for everything."

"I'll be in touch real soon," Jimmy said.

It was in Cuba where the palm tree grew. Jimmy sat facing away from the table, head bent to the Colt, turning it in his hand. Cuba a long, long time ago. Ten years after the Spanish-American War. No, he'd have to make it fifteen years after, because John Browning had not even made a prototype of the Colt before '09. The man who originally owned the gun, Colonel Hawes Rutherford, had been posted as a captain to Havana in 1901, where he served as an interpreter…Interpreter, Jimmy decided, wasn't enough of a job for Colonel Rutherford. He had to be a powerful man, or else he wouldn't be able to manipulate people the way Jimmy wanted. A liaison, then, between various American missions and the Cuban government. That would do the trick.

Over the course of a decade, thanks to his nefarious dealings with the corrupt Cuban officialdom, Colonel Rutherford amassed considerable wealth and power; and in 1910, following hard upon his promotion to colonel, recognizing that his position required a suitable companion, he returned to his native Virginia and presented himself at the plantation home of Mr. Morgan Lisle — where his father had worked the fields as a sharecropper — pursuant to seeking the hand of the Lisle's youngest daughter, Susan.

Jimmy stretched out his legs, cradling the Colt on his belly, and stirring the possibilities around. He believed Colonel Rutherford should have some leverage over the Lisles — he wasn't sure why yet, but the narrative absence where that leverage would fit felt like a notch in a knife edge, a place that wanted grinding and smoothing. He did not use logic to resolve the problem, just kept on stirring and letting his thoughts circulate. The character of Susan Lisle pushed forward in his mind, shaping herself and her circumstance from the whirled-up materials of the story, and as she grew more clearly defined, he came to understand what the leverage should be.

Mr. Lisle, a gentleman alcoholic renowned for his profligacy and abusive temper, had squandered most of the family fortune in a number of ill-considered business ventures, and the prospect of a marriage between Susan and Colonel Rutherford seemed to him, despite the colonel's lack of pedigree, a fine idea in that it served to rid him of an expense, and most pertinently, because the colonel had offered substantial loans with which Mr. Lisle might renew his inept assault upon the business world. And so it was that the marriage was arranged and celebrated, whereupon the colonel then whisked Susan away to Havana, to an elegant two-story house of yellow stucco with a tile roof and extensive grounds where flourished palms, hibiscus, bougainvillea, bananas, mangos, ceiba trees, and bamboo.

At the age of twenty-four, Susan Lisle Rutherford was an extraordinarily beautiful woman with milky skin and dark hair and blue eyes the color of deep ocean water. She was also a woman for whom the twentieth century had not yet dawned, having been nurtured in a family who clung stubbornly to the graces, manners, and compulsions of the antebellum period. In effect, by marrying at the urging of her parents, she had merely exchanged one form of confinement for another, emerging from the cloistered atmosphere of the plantation only to be encaged in a luxurious prison of Colonel Rutherford's design. Since the ceremony, she had not had a single day she cared to remember. The colonel was a stern, overbearing sort who kept her fenced in by spying friends and loyal servants and tight purse strings. She had not grown to love him, as her mother had promised she would, but to hate him. His demands of her in the marriage bed, though basic, had become a nightmarish form of duty. For nearly five years, she had been desperate, depressed, prone to thoughts of suicide. Not until recently had any glint of light, of life, penetrated the canopy of the colonel's protective custody.

Aside from the odd official function, Susan was permitted no more than three trips away from the house each week. Each Sunday she attended church in the company of the colonel's housekeeper Mariana, a stately bulk of a woman with light brown skin. Tuesday afternoons she went to market with Porfirio, the colonel's chef, and on Thursday evenings, escorted by the colonel's driver, Sebastian, she would make an appearance at the weekly dinner given by the president's wife for the wives of American and Cuban staff officers.

The dinner was held in a small banquet room at the Presidential Palace and was sometimes attended by other family members—it was on ŏne such occasion that Susan struck up a conversation with Arnulfo Carrasquel y Navarro, the nephew of General Oswaldo Ruelas, currently employed by the Banco Nacional but soon, he informed Susan, to become the owner of an export company dealing primarily in rum and tobacco. Ordinarily Susan would have been reluctant to speak with such a handsome young man, knowing that Sebastian reported her every movement to the colonel. But Sebastian had formed a romantic attachment with one of the palace maids; after leaving his charge at the banquet room door, he hurried off to meet his girlfriend. Thus liberated, Susan...

✦

"Excuse me!" Someone tapped Jimmy on the shoulder, making him jump. A tall middle-aged man with a bushy brown mustache, wide shoulders and an erect bearing, he wore a gray sport coat over a polo shirt. His face was squarish, a bit lantern jawed, and his brow scored by what struck Jimmy as three regulation furrows, each the same wavy shape as the one above or below, like an insignia of rank in some strange army. He smiled broadly and stuck out his hand. "Raymond Borchard," he said, sounding each letter in every syllable, as if expecting Jimmy might have a need to spell the name.

Jimmy didn't care for being interrupted in the middle of a story, but he supposed he had no one to blame but himself for working on it in a public place. He gave Borchard a limp hand so as to minimize what he presumed would be a serious massaging.

"I want to inquire about a gun," Borchard said. "The very gun you're holding, as a matter of fact."

Jimmy looked down at the Colt. "You after a Nineteen-Eleven, you can find one cheaper somewheres else."

"I believe," Borchard said, "that's Bob Champion's Colt."

"Sure is."

"I'd like to buy it."

"Well, that's good to hear," said Jimmy. "But it just now come to me, and I ain't had time to check it out...figure what it's worth. None of that."

"Four thousand," said Borchard. "You won't do better than four."

"Hell you say!" Jimmy said testily. "You ain't a dealer. You don't have a clue what I can get."

Borchard was big boned and thick waisted, and he surely went six-four, six-five. A man, by Jimmy's estimation, accustomed to having his way. The Borchard smile quivered, as if it was a strain to hold. A sharpness surfaced in his polished baritone, like a reef showing at low tide. "I apologize," he said. "I'm not usually so disrespectful. Chalk it up to eagerness."

Jimmy opened a display case and laid the Colt in beside a dueling pistol fancied by gold filigree and an engraved plate on the grip.

Borchard spread his hands, inviting Jimmy to take his best shot. "Now you know how much I want the Colt, why not seize the advantage and name your price?"

"'Cause like I said, I ain't had time to figure a price." Jimmy locked the display case.

"Six thousand." The Borchard smile had vanished.

"Six? This here gun must really make your eagle big." Jimmy patted the case that contained the Colt. "Wonder how much you'll want it tomorrow?"

Borchard folded his arms and stood there like he was Captain Authority without his crimefighter's costume and mask. "I gather from your attitude you've heard of me."

"Hasn't everybody? Major Ray Borchard's a damn household word where I hail from."

By the uncertainty in Borchard's face, Jimmy suspected that the major wasn't sure whether or not to accept this statement as fact.

"You don't much like me, Mister Guy. Is it my politics?"

"Naw, I deal with your kind all the time."

"My kind?" Borchard chuckled. "And what kind is that?"

"Wanna-bes." Jimmy locked the case, pocketed the key. "Old guys jerking off in the woods with twenty-man redneck armies and dreaming about world domination. Folks like you make up a good piece of my business."

"Then why not sell me the Colt?"

Jimmy had to admit the man had control. Anger was steaming off him like stink from a sewer grating, but his voice kept steady.

"She told you not to sell it to me," Borchard said. "Isn't that right?"

"She?"

Borchard let his eyes roll up toward the fluorescents, as if seeking guidance. "I'm beginning to think you're a fool, Mister Guy."

"I ain't the one who's offering six grand for a piece-of-shit gun belongs to some trailer-trash Robin Hood."

Borchard's sigh implied that Jimmy failed to understand both the vast powers arrayed against him and the grand truth of which he, the major, was representative. "I'll be back tomorrow," he said. "Perhaps by then you'll have assigned a price to the Colt."

"Gee, I don't know. Here you come offering six thousand. I better get me a second opinion before I move it. Might be worth way more'n I thought."

"Tomorrow," said Borchard sternly. "I want that gun."

"I will try hard not to dream about you," Jimmy said. "But I know I will."

His story mood was broken, and after Borchard had gone he busied himself by cleaning the glass of the display cases. He wished he could have gotten past the conversation between Susan and Arnulfo Carrasquel before Borchard showed up. Conversations weren't his strong suit, and he'd been on a roll. All in all, except for the Colt, it had been a shitty day, from arguing with Rita on down.

Arnulfo. He sounded the name under his breath. It didn't feel right. Something more familiar might be preferable. Manuel. Carlos. Luis. Luis Carrasquel. He couldn't make up his mind. Maybe, he thought, the thing to do would be to get someone to watch the tables and go grab one of those corn dogs. Food might settle him, put him back in the mood to work on the story. He was searching around for someone who wasn't busy at their own table, when he saw the Russians coming back.

Lucius Shepard

*

Brandywines was an ersatz English tavern with a sign above the door that depicted Henry the Eighth hoisting a cold one. Inside, there were paneled walls and waitresses in serving-wench costumes and black candleholders centering the oak tables, casting a dim light throughout, and a menu that advertised dishes such as Ye Olde Cheddar Melt and Steak Cromwell, a reference that probably eluded most diners. Not the sort of place Rita usually did her drinking, but the owner was hardcore NRA and had special prices for gun people. It looked like half the dealers in the show had folded early and were packed in around the bar. Several called out to her and waved, but nobody invited her over, which was how she wanted it. She flopped into a chair at a table next to the johns and told a chubby blond with pushed-up tits swelling from her peasant blouse to bring two Jack Black doubles neat, a Miller draft, and some fresh peanuts. While she was waiting for the drinks, a heavyset Latino wearing a Freitas Knives & Guns T-shirt, came out of the men's room, still in the process of zipping up. He caught her eye, grinned, and said, "Hey, Rita! How's business?"

"Fucking sucks, Jorge," she said. "How about you?"

The man shrugged. "About average for a Friday. But we'll get that heavy Labor Day action. We'll do all right." He appeared to expect a response, so Rita said, "Yeah, well," and looked blankly at him until he hitched up his pants, said, "See ya," and left her alone.

The first whiskey evened her out, the second made her feel almost sociable. She regretted having blown Jorge off. She wanted to bitch about Jimmy to someone. She'd say, I walk back over to the show, or the Red Roof, or wherever the hell he is, I'm going to find him setting there looking all moony-eyed at the Colt, telling himself one of his stories. I ain't saying the stories don't mean nothin'. It's how he gets out what he has to, and it's what what I need from him. I just wish he'd pay more attention to sales. Then Jorge would say,

He's a flake. So what? C'mon, Rita! The man baits a big sale better than anybody on the circuit. It's the nature of your business to go up and down more than most. You want steady, do like me and sell two, three hunnerd dollar weapons…Talking that way would make her feel even better. The Colt, now. That was a whole other ocean to swim in. The Colt and the story might cause them trouble, but they always skated through that kind of trouble. So long as she kept her hand on the controls, they'd be okay.

The waitress brought two more doubles. Rita sipped her whiskey and considered whether they should do the North Bend show or take a break till Yakima. It all depended on whether Jimmy sold the Beretta.

"Ms. Whitelaw?"

A tall white man with a thick mustache was smiling down on her; at his elbow, a younger guy with brushcut whitish blond hair and a pink cherub mouth that looked as if it had been transplanted from some Italian angel painting to an otherwise apelike face. The big man offered his hand. Rita said, "You keep it. I don't want it."

He continued to smile. "I was speaking to your partner about an hour ago."

The two of them. Like scoutmaster and scout. They pleased her, according with her take on white male orthodoxy. "Yeah?" she said. "What'd you think?"

"What did I think?"

"About Jimmy. What you think about the boy?"

The men exchanged a glance that Rita read as plain as if it were a sign saying We Got Us A Drunk Indian.

"To tell you the truth," the big man said, sitting down opposite her, "I found him somewhat shortsighted."

"Somewhat shortsighted." She rolled the phrase around. "That don't say it all, but I can't argue."

The young guy ducked into the chair beside the big man and sat still. The slyness of the move signaled to Rita that he thought he was doing something of which his leader might disapprove.

"I offered him four thousand for a Colt Nineteen-Eleven, and he turned me down flat," said the big man. "I hoped we—you and I—might discuss an arrangement."

She shook a finger at him, trying to dredge up the name. "The major. Borchard. I bet that's you."

"Raymond Borchard," he said after a pause. "I suppose Loretta Snow told you about me."

An uproar of laughter from the bar snagged Rita's attention. Cory Sauter of Sauter's Gifts and Guns was preparing to moon the establishment, standing with his pants held just below waist level, displaying the crack of his ass to a tableful of dealers, one of whom was holding up a fork, threatening to add of chunk of Cory's butt to his chef's salad.

"Loretta Snow," said Borchard impatiently. "She told you things about me, didn't she?"

"If she's a little white hen goes around clucking to herself and getting weepy…" Rita said. "Yeah, that'd be her."

Borchard's right eyelid drooped as if he were lining up a sight, and his smile was sucked into his mustache. Rita had the thought he didn't much care for anyone speaking ill of sweet Loretta. Which was odd, when you took into account the hen's attitude toward him.

"Plump little thing," Rita said. "You wouldn't need to grease the pan, you wanted to fry her up."

"I'd like to talk about the gun," Borchard said.

"Talk." Rita started on her fourth whiskey.

"I'll give you five thousand for it. Here and now."

She scooped up a handful of peanuts, tipped her head back and dribbled a few into her mouth. "Jimmy handles the buying," she said after swallowing.

"And just what do *you* handle, honey?" said the younger guy in a suggestive tone.

Borchard jumped on him hard. "Randy! I'll deal with this!"

Randy dropped his head and glowered at Rita through his albino eyebrows.

Rita said to the major, "Don't go punishing your bitch on my account. Doesn't matter what he says, I couldn't think no less of you."

Borchard leaned back, gauging her. "I realize Loretta must have poisoned the well, but in fairness, I'd like you to hear my side of things."

"Don't have nothing to do with *Loretta*." Rita gave the name a frilly emphasis. "I just can't stand white people."

The jukebox was plugged in, starting up at the midpoint of "Glory Days" so loud it obliterated all hope of conversation. Cries of protest, and the box was turned down.

"And yet," Borchard said, "you're involved with a white man, are you not?"

"Jimmy's not your typical Caucasian. He has visions, y'know. Kinda like my people."

Randy spat out a disdainful noise. The major stared him down, then reestablished his smile for Rita. "I thought he was a bit slow. I was hoping you were the brains of the outfit. Just goes to show."

Rita finished her beer and held up the empty glass as the blond waitress passed.

"Five thousand cash," said Borchard.

"That Colt must be big juju. Make it ten, I'll see what I can do."

"Goddamn it!" Randy slapped the table and gave Borchard a challenging look. "You going to let a fucking red nigger squaw treat us this way?"

"Better hush, Randy," Rita told him. "Daddy won't let you play with his machine gun no more."

Borchard turned on Randy. "Wait for me in the truck!"

"Jesus Christ, Ray! I was…"

"Wait in the truck!"

"What I tell ya?" Rita said as Randy got to his feet. "You in the shit for real now, bubba."

As Randy disappeared into the crowd, Rita said, "Probably too late for that child. Don't expect there's much can help him."

Borchard rested his elbows on the table. "You can't get five thousand for the Colt anywhere else. If Loretta told you not to sell to me, I'll arrange a third-party purchase. But before we discuss that, I want to tell you about Loretta. She's a good woman, but she knows how to manipulate men. I believe she's manipulating your Jimmy. Using him against me. We were involved, and..." He shook his head regretfully, leaving room for a response; when none came, he said, "Well?"

"What I just tell you? It's not my call."

The waitress returned, set down a draft and another double. She pointed at the double, beamed at Rita and said, "This one's on me, sweetie." Rita fished some folded bills from her shirt pocket, peeled off a ten and gave it to her. "'Case I forget later," she said.

"I thought you didn't like white people," said Borchard.

"I got a soft spot for the ones bring me whiskey."

The babble in the place washed over them. Shrieks of laughter mixed in with sports arguments, gun talk, people telling stories. By Saturday night some wouldn't be so happy. They'd have complaints about how the show was being run, business worries. Friday nights were always the best. The nostalgic quality of these thoughts did not trouble Rita as ordinarily they might. Four whiskeys, and she felt at home anywhere.

"I intend to have that Colt, Ms. Whitelaw," Borchard said.

"Talk to Jimmy."

"I'm talking to you." He leaned forward, his hands sliding across the table to invade her space, fingers close to touching her. "You have no idea the pressure I can bring to bear."

Anger rose in Rita like mercury in a hot glass stick. "I'd advise you to move your fucking hand," she said, "or you going to have to bring it back nine fingered." Borchard moved, and she rubbed the beer glass against her forehead until the desire to cut him abated.

"I've offered you a fair price," Borchard said. "I'm past the bargaining stage. I want that gun."

Given the major's passion for the Colt, the hen's passion not to sell it to him, and Jimmy's way of making his stories, Rita figured she knew more or less where he might be going with his newest one. She wondered where it would take her.

"I understand where you're coming from," she said to Borchard. "You look at me, you see this tough Indian woman's been through it. Reservation bred. Some shithole like Browning. She's learned how to take care of herself. Could be she got a hunting knife in her boot…and could be she's used it. But she's a known quantity. You believe you talk some shit to her, she'll recognize where her interests lie."

Borchard shifted in his chair, attentive.

"Jimmy, now, he ain't so easy to read. You say he's slow, but he's smart. It's just he was raised up hard by his daddy, and all his smartness got squashed over into one place in his head. He takes people he meets, fixes 'em up so they sound different and puts 'em in these stories he makes up. Beautiful stories! Doesn't write them down or nothing, but he remembers every goddamn word. You look at him, you see a spaced-out 'billy who's crazy for guns. But he goes a mile deeper'n that. I don't even know for sure what all's down in there."

"I'm sure he's brilliant," said Borchard. "What does that have to do with the Colt."

"I got two kids," Rita said. "I board them with my aunt, but they was with me around the time when I was getting to know Jimmy. Before we got together. So one night I was going out and I couldn't find nobody to stay with the kids. Jimmy volunteered. Appeared he could handle a couple preschoolers. So I left them fed and in their nightgowns. I got home, I found he'd taken his industrial stapler and stapled them up by their nightgowns to the wall. He'd spreadeagled the both of 'em to the boards like trophies. They'd been pestering him and he just couldn't deal with it. Course they kept on pestering him. They loved hanging on the walls, and they were running him ragged, getting him to

25

fetch sodas and candy." She laughed. "I was pissed, but I had to admit it was funny as hell."

"And your point is? Aside from warning me to keep clear of his stapler?"

"You'd do better to lay off pressuring Jimmy, 'cause inside he ain't nothing but pressure. You can't never tell what's gonna come out. He's one bottle cap you don't wanna pop."

Borchard gave his smile a rest and fixed her with a firm look intended, Rita thought, to convey the notion that his position was unshakable. "I want to give you five thousand for a weapon that isn't worth more than two," he said. "You can't walk away from that. And you can't jack me up any higher."

"I could show you a hole in the ground," Rita said, "and tell you there was a bear trap set at the bottom—I bet you'd still jump in to see if I was lying."

Borchard seemed pleased, as if he thought she'd paid him a compliment. "Going halfway gets you nowhere."

"Rita?"

A bearded man in a leather vest and plaid shirt was standing beside them; sheltering beneath his arm was a weary-looking woman with short gray hair and pronounced crow's-feet, clutching a menu to her chest.

"Mind if we join ya?" the bearded man asked. "If you're not talking business, that is. Isn't anywhere else to sit, and Mom's been on her feet all day."

"Sure thing, Doug. We're done." Rita scooched in her chair so they could slip past behind.

Borchard heaved up to his feet. "I tried," he said, projecting rueful menace, as if to convey that he was sorry things had reached this pass, but he wasn't the one who would suffer. "I guess I'll have to try harder."

"A little harder might be all it takes," Rita told him.

"Who's that you talking to?" Doug asked as Borchard moved off toward the door. Mom was occupied in studying the burger page of Ye Royal Board.

With Borchard gone, the tension caused by his presence removed, the whiskey kicked in full, and Rita felt a giddy buzz. "Just some character," she said. "I call him 'the major.'"

✦

Room 322 at the Red Roof Inn had a worn gray shag carpet, dull red drapes, a table by the door with two chairs, and a blond dresser supporting a three-piece mirror in which a queen-sized bed was reflected. But Jimmy, lying on the bed in his shorts, the Colt resting on his chest, saw in his mind's eye Susan Rutherford's bedroom in Havana, where she lay, among silk pillows and lace curtains and dark Spanish furniture, in the arms of her lover, Luis Carrasquel. Luis was a problem—Jimmy had no sense of the character. He was coming to recognize that Luis was more of a mechanism, and he didn't approve of characters who functioned only as mechanisms. However, in this instance he didn't seem to have much of a choice. Every time he tried to flesh Luis out, it felt wrong, and he was beginning to think there might be another character who would fill the slot that he had presumed Luis would fill. It was Susan's reaction to Luis, the colors it added to her perception of the world, that most mattered at this stage of things…

From their first delicately allusive conversation at the Presidential Palace, through a cautious, painfully attenuated courtship, through all their anxious and clandestine meetings, to the period in which they now existed, grown bold in their affections thanks to Colonel Rutherford's weekly trips to Guantanamo…Through every second of their affair, Susan had not experienced the slightest doubt that this lithe, clever, brown-skinned man was intended for her by God. His playfulness; his quickness of mind; his attentiveness at love; these qualities were in such opposition to her husband's controlling personality, his clumsy, often brutish sexual habits, she sometimes believed Luis had been sent her less as a lover than as a remedy. She was happier than she had ever been, so absorbed in the moment that she failed to consider the possible consequences of her actions. At the outset she had assumed that she and Luis would be married, but as the affair developed she came to understand the difficulties that would attend divorcing a man who wielded so much influence. Luis was protected to a degree by his family connections, but if nothing else, the colonel could destroy his business and cause him to be disgraced. Then there was the effect upon her family. In the event of a divorce action, the colonel would assuredly call in those loans made to her father, and that would result in her family's ruin. Thus it was at the moment of her great liberation, Susan recognized that her prison had only become more complex, more difficult to bear. Thanks to the intensity and sweetness of her lovemaking with Luis, her loathing for the colonel's embrace grew more pronounced. She had never been responsive to him, merely submissive. However, since the beginning of her relationship with Luis, she had taken to resisting the colonel's advances, and he in turn had taken to forcing her, both by physical means and by exploiting her feelings of powerlessness. Luis had announced that he was willing to endure whatever vengeance the colonel chose to exact, if Susan would come away with him; but she could not bring herself to harm so many people for a purpose as meager as that of her own happiness. And further, she had been brought up according to a tradition in which a wife's obedience to her husband was deemed a sacred article of the marriage contract, and despite Colonel Rutherford's insensitivity and abuse, she could not entirely escape the notion that *he* was the one who had been wronged.

Luis, who loved Susan as fervently as she did him, became increasingly desperate, yet found no outlet for his desperation. What, after all, could he do? She refused to allow him to confront the colonel, and he could not find it in himself to go contrary to her wishes. The idea of creating a circumstance that would bring the colonel to ruin occurred to him, as did that of murder. But he lacked sufficient guile to achieve the one, and had not been able to rouse in himself the brutality necessary to accomplish the other. For Susan's part, she knew that if she could not step away from her vows, then she ought to break things off with Luis. The pain she saw in his face was reason enough to sever the relationship, but she could not summon up the courage to deprive herself of the one thing that gave her joy, that breached the joyless confinement of the marriage. She told Luis on several occasions that it would be best for him if they ended the affair, but each time he begged her to reconsider and each time she relented. She realized that to continue as they were in the face of her indecisiveness was foolhardy. But desire and love were proof against understanding, and they went on as before.

Whenever the colonel traveled out from Havana, Luis would wait until eleven in the evening to scale the western wall of the estate. Once he had gained the top of the wall he would chin himself onto the lowermost branch of an enormous ceiba tree and climb through the canopy, which spanned the distance between the street and the house. From the eastern edge of the canopy, he could swing out and clutch the vines that enmeshed the yellow stucco and thus he was able to climb to Susan's bedroom window. As Susan was in the habit of locking her door, except on those occasions when the colonel announced that he would be visiting her chambers, she and Luis would then be safely hidden away until the early morning. His leave-taking, however, was not so easily managed, for the branches of the ceiba beneath Susan's window would not support the weight of someone leaping down onto them. Thus he was forced to descend to the lawn by means of the vines and make his way through the thick shrubbery to the western wall. This course had one particular point of peril. To reach the shrubbery he had to pass a doorway at the rear of the house, in front of which a sapling sabal palm had recently been transplanted. The door led to a staircase that ascended into the body of the house and, fur-

29

ther along, to the apartments inhabited by the colonel's housekeeper Mariana. It was frequently left ajar, since Mariana — a light sleeper — was given to waking in the night and going out for a stroll; she did not always shut the door on her return. But because she was a creature of regular habits, bathing each morning between five-thirty and six, Luis was able to time his exits so as to coincide with her ablutions...

✦

The door to Room 322 was pushed open, breaking the glide of Jimmy's thoughts, and Rita came in. For a moment he had trouble focusing on her, still immersed in the story. The Colt resting on his chest felt warm, like a heavy pat of melting butter. Rita tossed her key onto the table by the door and sat in one of the chairs and began shucking off her boots. Jimmy could tell she was drunk by the cautious precision of her movements.

"Y'all have fun?" he asked.

She made a sardonic noise with teeth and tongue. "Oh yeah. Brandywines...it was just like Mardi Gras."

"I moved the Beretta," he said.

She looked up. "Full price?"

"I gave him a cash discount. Ten percent."

"He paid cash? No shit!"

"Yeah. He took one of them fancy oak and velvet boxes, too. And I got a nibble on the Colt."

"How's that?"

"I borrowed Bob Ochuda's laptop and sent an e-mail to that professor at Washington State. Guy who bought the Waco rifle. I told him we had Bob Champion's personal sidearm. He got real excited. Says he's going to come see us in North Bend." Jimmy laid the Colt aside. "We oughta look into getting us a laptop. I feel bad borrowing Bob's all the time."

Rita tossed her right boot toward the bed, set the hunting knife she kept in it next to the keys, then went to working on the left boot. "You are one slick white boy, Jimmy. Guess I gotta learn to trust ya."

"You always say that," he said. "And about half the time you wrong."

She laughed, the first honest laugh he'd had from her in days. "Damn!" she said. "Here I been drinking to drown my sorrows, and now I'm wishing I had a drink to celebrate."

He pointed to the dresser. "Top right-hand drawer."

One booted, she stepped to it, opened the drawer, and plucked out a pint of Jack Black. She went into the bathroom, reappeared a few seconds later with a water glass half full of whiskey. She leaned against the doorframe and sipped. "That was nice, Jimmy. Thinking about me like that."

"I spend all the time I got to spare thinking about you."

She returned to the chair, placed the glass and the bottle on the table, started in again on her boot.

"So what'd you do at Brandywines?"

"Sat with Doug Lindsey and his mama for a while. He's trying to tell me we oughta carry custom ammo for the antique pieces. I ain't so sure he's wrong."

"We don't need the inventory. I mean, hell, we could carry a coupla boxes that fit with some of the pieces. But we doing okay without it."

Rita kicked off the boot, sailed it into the bathroom. "Ever see Doug's mama eat? That scrawny little thing wolfed down two of them half-pounder cheeseburger-and-steak-fry plates. Woman must have the metabolism of a racehorse." She began undoing the buttons of her shirt. "Ran into that major the Snow woman told us about."

"Yeah, I had a conversation with him over to the show."

"He offered five thousand cash for the Colt."

Jimmy grinned. "Offered me six."

"Huh. He probably thought I was desperate for firewater. Anybody smiles as much as that bastard's got a snake coiled in his belly." She had another drink. "Maybe we should take the six and skim two grand off the top."

"C'mon, Rita. You know you just talking."

"You didn't sell the Beretta, I wouldn't be just talking." She drained her glass and poured another two fingers. "How's the story going?"

"All right, I guess. Wanna hear?"

"Sure I do."

As he talked she lifted her butt, slid her jeans down past her knees, then her ankles, and sat there in shirt and panties, sipping whiskey. The Painted Desert color of her body flowed into his eyes, adding a dark red wash to the air. He could see the story molding itself to her lean figure, adding vigor and heat. This was the heart of what they were together, the blood of the relationship, the cracked moon that shined them into being. Him telling, her listening and giving advice. The spirit they became in the process. He felt energy bridging between them, arcs of tropical lightning, gun flashes welded into a current, scattered drumbeats collecting into a roll. The words yielded a mysterious glow as they fell around her, like fading fireworks.

"Where'd you learn that Cuban stuff?" she asked after he had finished.

"Some's from books, and Daddy told me some. He was with the Marines in Guantanamo."

"Least the son of a bitch did you one favor before he checked out."

A truck engine turned over in the parking lot, its idle rumbling like a sleepy monster, and somebody let out a sharp shout like they had spotted it and were afraid.

"How much more you got?" she asked.

"I figured out most everything except the ending. Y'know, the endings always give me trouble."

"You need to put some more in about the major."

"The colonel," he said. "Not the major."

"Y'gotta grow him realer than the other two."

"Susan's real," he said, defensive.

"Saying she's kept down ain't enough. You gotta show what's doing it to her. You gotta make it so he's the strongest thing in the story."

"Maybe...I don't know."

"I'm telling ya. He should be your story...least there should be more of him in the first part. You need to do something with Susan, too."

Depressed now, Jimmy said, "Don't sound like you enjoyed it so much."

"Well, there ain't a whole lot *to* enjoy right now. Just a couple of characters. But it's got potential...and you tell it real nice."

The word "nice" sounded to Jimmy like the click of washer in a blind man's begging cup.

Rita went to the dresser, where she'd set the pint, and poured herself another three fingers. She leaned against the dresser and crossed her legs. Folded her arms. She gazed at Jimmy fondly, and he dropped his eyes to her legs.

"It reminds me of them romances my aunt's all the time reading," she said. "You should make it meaner'n that. It's a mean story."

"I was thinking it's a love story."

"Most love stories got some meanness in 'em."

"I suppose," he said sullenly.

"Look at the colonel—he's mean." Rita had a swallow of whiskey, let it settle. "Meanness begets meanness. Maybe Susan's got to get a little mean herself. 'Less you gonna let her just lay there and take it, and that ain't right. Even a weak woman's got teeth."

He tried to come up with a way to satisfy her and still do what he wanted, but couldn't fit everything together.

"I'm the one you're telling the story to," Rita said, "and all I'm saying is, I ain't interested in a woman ain't got a backbone. A man does her wrong, she oughta do him the same. I can't respect nobody just rolls over and says, 'Do it again.'"

When you changed one thing, you changed everything. The elements of Jimmy's story drifted apart, becoming vague and unrelated to any other, like the tag-ends of dreams whose meaning he couldn't recapture. Rita was staring at him expectantly, but he felt stupefied, unable to turn what he was thinking into words.

"Well, do what you want," she said diffidently, and started for the bathroom. "I'm gonna wash up."

Jimmy lay for a time with his eyes half-closed, fingering the Colt, rubbing a raised patch on the housing. It was cold now, just a gun, not the warm touchstone it became when he was reeling off the story. Took the story to tickle it to life.

"Wake up!" said Rita.

She was standing naked at the foot of the bed like a savage female spirit who'd walked into a dream he was having. Her small high-riding breasts and long-muscled thighs were baked to a hard pottery gloss. Covering her right breast and part of her ribcage was a tattoo depicting a red and purple serpent with hands who looked to be standing on its tail and holding out an apple. It was real good work. The style was old-fashioned, kind of like a nineteenth century engraving, but the colors were bright. Down below, she was shaved hairless.

"Uh-oh," he said. "How much trouble am I in?"

She cocked her left hip, rested a hand on it. "Trouble don't even say it."

✦

Friday night had been unkind to Loretta Snow. As she approached the Guy'Guns table at ten o'clock the next morning, no more than a minute or two after the doors had opened, she fiddled with her purse strap, cast nervous glances to the side, and appeared generally unsteady. The bruised-looking skin beneath her eyes was darker and puffier; her buttermilk complexion had acquired a gray undertone. Jimmy thought she looked pretty nonetheless, wearing an ankle-length cotton print with an Empire waist. Rita, who was badly hungover, moaned when she saw the woman coming and laid her head down on a display case. Jimmy got to his feet and smiled and said, "Morning."

Without pleasantry or preamble, Ms. Snow said, "I need to have my gun back." She held out a hand like a child demanding a quarter.

"I ain't even put it on display," said Jimmy, disconcerted.

"I'm sorry." Ms. Snow's chin trembled. "I need it back."

"Well, it's your gun, but I think you rushing things." Jimmy came out from behind the table, hitched his thumbs in his back pockets. "Man's traveling down from Pullman to look at it next week. You might get your four outa him. Maybe a little more."

She perked up for a second, hearing that, but then seemed to shrink down inside herself. "I can't wait that long."

"I'll give it to you," he said. "That's not a problem. But you oughta hear about this fella before you jump. Whyn't we grab us a cup of coffee, and I'll fill you in? You want the Colt back after, I'll hand her over."

She hesitated. "All right. But I don't know if anything can change my mind."

Rita's head was still down. Jimmy bent close to her and said, "Need you to watch the table for a half-hour. Okay?"

"Just give her the damn gun," she said wearily, voice muffled by her arm.

He put his mouth to her ear and whispered, "I ain't finished my story! You can handle the table. Hardly anybody's here."

She flapped a hand at him. "Go on."

"Want me bring you back something?"

"Bring me a fucking cure for pain," she said.

Jimmy steered Ms. Snow by the elbow along the empty aisles, past dealers slumped in folding chairs behind mounds of T-shirts, some gazing bleakly at the walls, others lethargically sorting their change, or talking on cell phones, or rummaging through boxes of stock. Everyone in the show looked to be in about the same shape as Rita, except for Hardy and Rosalie Castin, a Christian couple who stood jauntily at the ready behind display cases arrayed with shiny new handguns and semi-autos and speed loaders, the good soldiers in an otherwise dissolute army. Once Jimmy had paid for the coffee, he and Ms. Snow found an unoccupied bench at the edge of the parking lot that faced toward a Key Bank and made themselves comfortable. The green humps of the Cascades lifted beyond the bank, their summits aglow in a sunstruck mist.

"This fella I told you about," Jimmy said, "teaches up at State and writes books about the white power movement and the militias. Few years ago he talked the university into funding a collection of memorabilia. I had this rifle I couldn't move. It was used by the Branch Davidians down there in Waco. Reason I couldn't move it, I didn't have much in the way of authentication. I had a letter from one of the cult members saying David Koresh had carried the rifle at one time, but collectors...they looking for a gun he used during the siege, and I wasn't able to get testimony to that effect."

"It sounds sick," Ms. Snow said in her milk-and-cookies voice.

"I can't deny there's that element. When I started the business, I didn't carry crime guns. But I learned I needed that market if I was gonna survive." He sipped his coffee, found it too sweet, and set the cup on the bench beside him. "This professor, Doctor Wylie, he ain't no sicko. Just a man with an obsession. And that's why he might be the fella'll give you four. He paid me a whole lot more'n that Davidian rifle was worth. Way he reacted to my e-mail, I figure he's hot for your Colt. I got no idea what he might pay, but since there ain't no question about its authenticity, I'm guessing four might be low." He smacked his forehead, as if to punish himself. "I shoulda thought of him yesterday, but it didn't occur to me till after you left."

Ms. Snow gazed off along the street. The traffic had picked up, and the parking lot was beginning to fill.

"See," Jimmy went on, "I can tell him Borchard's offered me six and that'll juice the price."

The major's name galvanized Ms. Snow. "I want the gun back," she said fretfully. "I'm sorry. I..."

She made to stand, but Jimmy caught her hand. "What's the matter?" he asked.

Ms. Snow's shoulders heaved and she leaked a sob. Her trouble pulled at Jimmy, tightened his chest — the same as he got whenever he watched TV by himself and they ran a commercial for starving kids you could feed on twenty dollars a month and he took to feeling sad not for just them, but for himself at being part of that world.

"Hey," he said. "It ain't nothing can't be fixed. Tell me what's wrong."

"You can't help me," she said, but there was an inch of hope in her voice.

"You need to tell somebody. That much is plain."

She cut her eyes toward him. They were a cold dark blue, like the water in the San Juan Straits on a sunny day. She made no effort to free her hand from his grasp.

"He came to see me last night," she said.

"Borchard?"

A nod. "He was furious. He told me to get the gun for him. He said you wouldn't sell it, and he wasn't going to allow Bob Champion's gun to pass into the hands of somebody didn't know its true value."

"Hell with him," Jimmy said.

"You don't understand! He's threatening me!"

"Call the police. They'll take care of him."

"The police won't do anything. He knows most of them. They all think he's Christ come down."

Jimmy started to say something, but Ms. Snow cut in and said tearfully, "You don't understand!"

The sliding door of an old green Dodge van in the lot opened and half a dozen teenage boys climbed out. They shuffled about moodily, not talking much, waiting on the driver to lock up. Sallow and unkempt, untrendily dressed in jeans and sweaters, none of which bagged. They moseyed off, two abreast, toward the entrance to the armory, a platoon of stragglers cut loose from some disenchanted force,

Lucius Shepard

maybe looking to arm themselves for an assault on homeroom tyrants, Nazi jocks. Ms. Snow eyed them warily.

"I ain't never gonna understand unless you explain it to me," Jimmy said.

She sighed, stared toward the bank. "We have a history, the major and I. I met him at church, and he seemed nice. I hadn't been out with anyone since Bob died. I guess I was lonely and not looking closely enough. We went out four times. It wasn't going anywhere. It just felt good getting away from the kids. Anyway, one day I found out he was in the movement. I've had all I can take of those people. When he came over that night I told him I wouldn't see him anymore. He started yelling and kicking the furniture. Some of the things he said made me realize the only reason he attached himself to me was that I used to belong to Bob Champion. That's how he put it. I 'belonged' to Bob. I think he may have been attracted to me the same way he's attracted to the gun." She toyed with the catch of her purse. "He kept getting madder and madder. The upshot of it all is, he forced me." She held Jimmy's eyes an instant, as though to establish that she had dealt with this and was unashamed.

"You report it?"

"Oh, yes. That's how I know the cops won't do anything. He told them I was hysterical because he'd broken it off with me. They weren't interested in a rape, they won't get out of their chairs if I report him for a threat."

Jimmy gave the situation a turn or two, and was distracted by an old Chrysler, an early fifties model, black and grumbling, that nosed into the slot directly behind the bench; the engine dieseled for a few seconds after the ignition had been switched off. A fat woman, as massive and all-over bulging as a sumo wrestler, with a head of dyed-black curls, squeezed from behind the wheel. She was cinched into stretch pants and a flowered smock. She gasped for breath and hauled a canvas-sheathed shotgun out from the trunk.

"What y'know, Shelly?" he called.

The woman saw him and a smile pumpkin-carved her flushed round face. "Hi there, Jimmy!" She waddled a couple of steps toward the bench, shouldering the shotgun. "Didn't think we'd be seeing you till Yakima."

He held up a hand, rubbed thumb and forefinger together to signify a need for cash.

"I hear that." She cast a suspicious glance at Ms. Snow. "Well, I'll talk to ya inside, awright?"

He waved, went back to studying the situation. Finally he said to Ms. Snow, "How much you tell Borchard about our deal?"

"Nothing, really. I said I gave you the gun to sell."

"Tell him you misspoke. Tell him you sold it to me."

"That won't stop him."

She had collected herself while relating her story, but now she began to unravel again, to mist up and twist the hem of her dress. Jimmy pictured her trying to cover herself with a torn blouse, while the colonel stood above her, arms folded, stern as a Viking statue, but weak...weak in his bones.

"We can get this done," Jimmy said.

"I don't see how."

"What he wants most is the Colt, right?"

"I suppose."

"And if you had the money, how soon could you leave for Seattle?"

"Tomorrow...if I *had* the money. We can stay with my cousin in Ballard till I find a place."

"Then it's easy. We'll write us a bill of sale. We'll go to a notary and get him to witness it's not a real sale. That's to protect you. I'll show the bill to the colonel if needs be, and I'll tell him I'll break my bond about not selling him the Colt so long as he leaves you alone. But I got another buyer. If he wants it, he has to bid."

"What if he says no?"

"What's he gonna do? Kill me? That wouldn't bring him the gun. Truth is, I doubt he's up to killing. He's a bully. A bully ain't gonna pick on a cat with claws."

"The major," said Ms. Snow.

He waited for her to finish.

"Before...you said 'the colonel.' It's major."

"Same difference," he said.

There was a shine on the Key Bank clock—he had to squint to see where the hands were pointing. Getting on eleven. Rita would be starting to squirm. By the time they returned from the notary, she would be ready to eat his liver. But he couldn't help that.

"I'm gonna call my professor," Jimmy said. "He finds out I got a buyer down here, he'll bid it up over the phone. I was you, I'd go home and pack. We might get this thing done by Labor Day."

A drop of suspicion added itself to her mix. "Why're you doing all this?"

"It ain't 'all this,'" he said. "I'm gonna make serious money. I let them bid it up, hell, the Colt might move for five figures. When two men think a gun means something, they can be extremely impractical."

He couldn't read her expression.

"Thank you," she said, and put her arms about his neck.

Her body eased up against him, and the hug lasted so long, Jimmy did not think it could be legally construed a hug. More of an embrace. It brought a character out from the shadows of his story, one with a new slant on the situation. A man. The character was gone too quickly for him to identify, but its brief appearance caused Jimmy to ignore the tension the hug had bred in him, and to become an active participant in the embrace, smelling Ms. Snow's hair, his right hand going to her waist. Her mouth grazed his cheek, skittered up to his ear.

"I don't believe you," she whispered.

✦

Rita wasn't mad like Jimmy had expected. She had moved a midrange piece and someone wanted to take a look at the gas-cylinder Thompson they kept locked in the van. It wasn't often she closed a sale, and it had boosted her spirits. She limited her displeasure with him to a disgruntled shake of the head. But when he told her he needed the van that evening to visit Borchard, she arched her back and spat.

"You messing with that white woman?" she asked. "Is that what this shit's about?"

"Christ, Rita." He brushed a scrap of candy bar wrapper off the top of a display case.

She reached across the table and punched his arm with the heel of her hand. "I saw you scoping her out. You wouldn't look no sharper, you'd been trying to guess her goddamn weight."

Somebody had left a book on the back corner of the table. *The Golden Age of Shotgunning.* He wondered when the Golden Age had been. Probably depended on where you were living.

Rita punched him again, harder, and a bubble of anger boiled up from the surface of his thoughts, as if something big down below was blowing its tanks, preparing to rise. "Fuck's wrong with you?" he said. "I'm trying to sell a gun and I'm working on a story. You know how I get. So leave me the fuck alone!"

Her eyes spiked him, but his anger was taller than hers for a change, or else she was too sick to fight. She sat looking into her partial reflection in the top of a display case. "I'm a real bitch this morning," she said. "I'm sorry, baby."

"You a bitch most of the damn time," he said. "Most of the time I kinda like it. But I could stand you easing off some today."

"I'm sorry." She reached out a hand, as if to touch him, but didn't complete the gesture. "Y'ain't messing with her, are ya?"

"Think I'd screw up what we got?"

"No. But you get tempted when you're telling a story. I know it's only part of the story, but it worries me."

"Nothing's gonna happen." His anger had subsided, but he couldn't jump down yet from the peak it had left him standing on.

"Maybe I'll go back to the motel and sleep for an hour," she said.

"Okay."

"Sure you can handle things?"

"Buncha assholes saying—" he did a cartoon voice "'—That really Teddy Roosevelt's gun?' I reckon I can handle that. It gets busy, I'll give you a call."

"All right."

She moved out into the aisle, then leaned across the table and kissed him, her tongue flirting briefly with his.

The kiss brought everything inside him back to even. "That a promise?" he asked.

"Not hardly, lover. That's a gift subscription."

By one o'clock the crowds had grown heavy, thick with teenage shoplifters and once-through gawkers. Jimmy propped his SERIOUS INQUIRIES ONLY sign against a display case, turned his chair sideways to the aisle, and sat holding the Colt in his lap. The buzz and mutter of the show seemed to be etching a pattern of static in his head, but the oil-smooth patina of the gun soothed him, and he fell to thinking about Colonel Hawes Rutherford, a big cold man, wide shoulders racked beneath his dress uniform, dark beard trimmed neat as a pencil sketch, standing beside the breakfast table, staring down at his wife's breasts, nestled in the lacy shells of a peignoir. The sight caused him frustration—he had not been with Susan for several weeks—and also inspired a feeling of disdain toward this display of female softness, the very same that provoked his arousal. He was happiest when focused upon affairs of duty, whether negotiating with the sublimely corrupt officialdom of the country or directing the movements of materiel. He perceived himself to be a soldier in the service of, first, order and then the United States, and it sometimes galled him that the rigor of his mental life should be diluted by an addiction to the feminine, with all its cryptic delicacy and attendant confusions. This inborn condescension aside, there was no doubt the colonel loved his wife, even respected her in some pale fashion. Women, he felt, were due respect for the exact reasons they deserved protection. That they were weak and sought to prevail in life spoke to an admirable persistence. As for love, the colonel had written a treaty with his brain, ceding a certain portion of his mental life to the nourishing of a smallish flame notable for its steadiness. Each day prior to returning home — or if he was away — before retiring he would think those thoughts he deemed essential to the maintenance of the flame, including appreciations of Susan's beauty and sense of style, her effectiveness at state functions, her efficiency in overseeing the servants, her fidelity. For the duration of the exercise he would faithfully put from mind those elements of her personality he found wanting. He excused his proprietary attitude toward Susan and the abuses that arose from it by countenancing them necessary in order to make the flower of her womanhood bloom, and on those rare occasions when he was confronted by the realization that he had misused her, he forgave himself — in his view, when it fell to an older man to instruct a young woman, the acts of instruction themselves were bound to stimulate certain primitive, albeit godly, desires, and he was nothing if not a natural man. So it was that he managed to sustain the self-image of an honorable, kindly, and loving husband, a far cry from the unfeeling, humorless monster Susan perceived him to be.

As he stood that morning gazing down at his wife's charms, his faith in this self-image caused him to dismiss all doubts relating to the fact that he knew Susan would likely not wish to hear what he intended to tell her. "My dear," he said. "I'll be leaving tomorrow for Guantanamo."

Susan, who was reading a letter from her mother, did not lift her eyes from the paper and murmured an acknowledgment.

"I would hope," the colonel went on, "to be received by you this evening."

It appeared to him that Susan flinched an instant before she whispered her assent, yet she offered no objection or excuse as she had done in the past. Feeling that he was making good progress with her, the colonel picked up his hat, bid her good day, and left the house.

While stopping in Santiago, on his way back from Guantanamo several days later, the colonel, having satisfactorily settled a thorny problem of miscommunication between the commandant of the base and a loose association of local fisherman, treated himself to a night at the house belonging to Sra. Amalia Savon, an establishment known more famously amongst the locals as Tia Maria's. The colonel almost never frequented such places, but on those occasions when he did he justified the indulgence by telling himself that the tutelage of a wise professional would serve to inform his own instruction of Susan. On this particular evening, after spending several pleasant hours with a young lady by the name of Serafina, he repaired to the downstairs bar where, in the company of several Cuban gentlemen, he helped himself to a large postcoital brandy and a good cigar. As he sat in a comfortable chair of red velvet in a quiet corner, nursing his brandy and less thinking than savoring the quality of his satisfaction, he was approached by a distinguished elderly man with a full head of white hair, wearing a cream-colored suit and walking with a malacca cane; he had in tow a much younger fellow, a reedy, sallow sort wearing fawn slacks and a yellow *guayabera*.

"Your pardon, Colonel Rutherford," said the elderly man with a bow. "I am Doctor Eduardo Lens y Rivera. You may recall that we met last April in Havana at the American Embassy. We had a brief discussion regarding the regulatory body that oversees imports into your great country."

"Of course! Doctor Lens!" The colonel's pleasure was genuine. Lens had struck him as a reasonable politician, an anomaly among his grasping, shortsighted colleagues.

"May I present my wife's cousin?" Doctor Lens indicated the younger man. "Odiberto Saenz y Figueroa."

"*Mucho gusto,*" said Odiberto, and shook the colonel's hand.

Once they had taken chairs adjoining his, the colonel said, "I apologize for not recognizing you straightaway, Doctor. I was..."

"Please!" Doctor Lens held up a hand to restrain the colonel's excuses. "There is no need to explain. Following an evening at Tia Maria's, a man tends to reorder his perspectives."

After further pleasantries, compliments all around to the women of Cuba, those of America, as well as various other Caribbean nations, Doctor Lens slid forward in his chair and rested both hands on the macaw-shaped gold head of his cane. "Colonel," he said, "there is something I wish to discuss with you, but I hesitate because it is a matter of considerable personal delicacy."

"Personal?" The colonel set his brandy down. "Personal in what way?"

"In the deepest and most fundamental way. It relates to your family."

"I'm afraid I have no real family," the colonel said. "My sister and parents have passed on. There is only my wife and..."

"Exactly," said Doctor Lens; then, after a pause: "Truly, colonel, I do not wish to offend. I bring this matter to your attention only because I would wish it brought to mine were our positions reversed."

"Let me get this straight. You have information concerning my wife?"

"Information is, perhaps, too strict a word. What I have is a story told by one young man to another. Young men are prone to boasting. All I can do is offer you the opportunity to hear the story and make your own judgment as to its authenticity. Should you not care to hear it, then I will beg your pardon and take my leave."

Shaken, the colonel curled his fingers round the brandy glass, but felt he did not have the strength to lift it. The idea that Susan had been unfaithful, and he could think of no other circumstance that would cause Doctor Lens to come forward in so oblique a fashion...It was insupportable, implausible, unfathomable. She would not be the first American wife to take a Cuban lover, but given her isolation and the inquisitive nature of his servants, he could not imagine how she would manage it.

"Go ahead," he said with some confidence.

"Do you know a man named Luis Carrasquel? The nephew of General Ruelas?"

"I know of him. We may have met...I'm not sure."

"Odiberto is employed the Banco Nacional, where Carrasquel also works. And that is not their sole association. They have been friends since childhood. Our families have vacationed together. A week ago, Carrasquel asked Odiberto to have a drink with him after closing. He seemed quite distraught and said that for some time he had been involved in a romance with a beautiful American woman. The woman loved him — he was certain of that. Yet for reasons he could not understand, she refused to leave her husband, a man she described — " Doctor Lens offered the colonel an apologetic look " — as a monster."

Colonel Rutherford suffered this slur without visible reaction. But a numbness began to spread from his extremities, and along with the numbness, though he rejected the notion that whatever their personal difficulties, Susan could ever think so badly of him as to call him a monster, there came a feeling of certainty that the story was no boast.

"I think it might be best if Odiberto told the story from this point on," said Doctor Lens. "I have heard it but once. Thus I cannot recall every detail...and it is from the details, I believe, that you will be able to determine its truth. Since Odiberto regrettably speaks no English, I will translate."

"That's fine," said the colonel, and favored Odiberto with what he intended as an encouraging smile.

The story unfolded in a curious fashion, alternating between Odiberto's bursts of passionate narration, accompanied by florid gestures and woeful faces, and the calm, almost lectoral translations of Doctor Lens. The emotional opposition of these two styles set up a dissonance in the colonel's thoughts, and it came to seem that he was listening to both a lie and the truth at once, and that at heart they were the same.

"I have never seen Luis so upset," said Doctor Lens. "Once we reached the bar, he began to cry. When I asked what was wrong, he said he could not tell me. He could tell no one, and the pressures of the situation were driving him mad. But at length I prevailed upon him to confess his secret. I swore I would never reveal it."

"Apparently this was not a sacred oath," the colonel said with wry bitterness.

Doctor Lens let out a heavy sigh. "It is shameful, I know. Odiberto's motives in coming forward were less than pure. He was passed over for promotion at the bank and blames this upon Luis, who is in a supervisory position. But since the story is out, I thought it best that you be made aware of things."

"When you say the story is out," the colonel said, "what do you mean? Has he told anyone else apart from you?"

"My wife," said Doctor Lens. "Odiberto told us together. I give you my word that I will tell no one, but my wife…" He shrugged. "I can control how much money she spends at market, but not whom she whispers to."

"I understand," said the colonel. "Please…proceed."

Odiberto, through the agency of Doctor Lens, told of the married woman's indecisiveness, this the thing that had caused Luis so much pain and distraction.

"He could not determine what she wanted," the doctor said. "One minute she was telling him she would do anything to make him happy, and the next she became distant, uncommunicative. He asked me what he should do, and I advised him to break it off. No matter how much he loved this woman, I said, it would be the act of a fool to surrender his life to what was on the face of it a hopeless passion. But Luis shook his head, said, 'No, no! There must be a way to make her know...to make her see...'

"He was fanatic in his devotion to the woman. Even obsessive. I could not convince him that he was on the road to disaster, that the physical, mental, and moral dangers he confronted were likely to destroy him. In hopes of finding some means of persuading him, I convinced to tell me more about the relationship."

Doctor Lens leaned forward and said in a lowered voice, "I will spare you the intimate details, if you wish."

"No," said the colonel, who felt cold and immobile, as though imprisoned within a block of stone. "No, I want to hear it all."

As he listened to Doctor Lens describe the woman's passion, the unalloyed freedom with which she employed her body in the service of her lover's pleasure, Colonel Rutherford began to take heart. This woman, with her unending avidity and sexual inventiveness...She could not be Susan. Either Carrasquel was lying, or he was describing someone else entirely. But then the doctor related how Luis gained entry to the estate. The ceiba tree, the sapling palm, the doorway leading to the housekeeper's apartments, the vines crawling over the yellow stucco. Only a single shred of doubt remained in the colonel's mind.

"Did Carrasquel ever speak this woman's name?" he asked.

After a hurried consultation with Odiberto, Doctor Lens said, "Several days following our initial conversation, Luis and I were walking in the market, taking our lunch *al fresco,* when Luis stopped to stare at pale beautiful woman who

was shopping with a servant. He appeared absolutely devastated by the sight. A moment later the woman lifted her
head and their eyes met. The exchange was not casual. For
the longest time they seemed unable to move away from one
another, and after the woman had left, in a great hurry, I
should say. After she left, Luis was beside himself. Flustered,
incoherent. His eyes filled with tears, and he refused to speak
other than to insist we return to the bank at once. I later as-
certained that the name of the woman who provoked this
reaction was Susan Rutherford."

The colonel lowered his eyes to the carpet. "Is there
more?" he asked grimly.

"Only this," Doctor Lens said. "And it is I, now, who
speak. I hope you will accept that I speak as a friend." He
fingered the beak of the gold macaw. "No one, not even General Ruelas, will blame you if you seek revenge for this be-
trayal. However, I beg you to be moderate in your judgment.
Not only are the lives of Carrasquel and your wife in the
balance, but your own. Should your vengeance be a bloody
one, your career may suffer. Cuba needs American friends
such as Colonel Hawes Rutherford."

These last words, imparted with a sly oiliness, made clear
to the colonel that Doctor Lens' motives in telling him the
story were, like Odiberto's, less than pure. The doctor wanted
something, and consequently, he must have something to
give. It occurred to the colonel that he was being subtly and
unobtrusively blackmailed—in effect, being offered *carte
blanche* as regarded his handling of the infidelity in return
for some favor yet to be determined.

"You say your wife cannot be controlled?" he asked.

"Not easily controlled, at any rate," said the doctor.
"Though I suppose it might be possible, with great effort, to
restrain her."

"And can you guarantee Odiberto's silence?"

"Odiberto understands that his revelation will only profit
him if " — the doctor appeared to be contemplating a choice
of words; then he smiled " — if there is profit to be had."

The colonel, in whom rage had begun to stoke its fires, could barely withhold from striking him. He had endured a sufficiency of these effete little men, these half-breeds with their dapper attire and usurers' hearts. But he only said, "I would very much appreciate it if you would do your level best to ensure your wife's discretion."

The doctor nodded, said, "Of course," as if no contrary thought had ever entered his mind.

"Perhaps," the colonel continued, "you will visit me in my office so we can discuss the matter further."

"I would be delighted," replied the doctor.

Once the two men had departed, the colonel knocked down his brandy and went out onto the grounds of Tia Maria's. He stood beneath a coconut palm, tipped back his head and gazed at the sky.

All the feelings he had suppressed during the conversation now came spilling out, like tiny devils bursting free from an enchanted box, led by Fury, but followed in swift order by Hate, Bitterness, Loathing, Envy, Despair, and, lastly, by a horrid, squirming, tumescent thing he could not identify by name, but that he recognized as emblematic of the odious and unhealthy sexuality that the news of Susan's infidelity had roused from his depths. These vile beasts of feeling enlarged him, inflated him with their gaseous breath, making him so great with emotion, he half-believed that were he to stretch out his hand, he might pluck the stars from out of their sockets of black bone and rewrite the diamond sentences of the sky to contrive a tale of calumny and murder. The colonel was not a courageous man. He had used his family connections to ensure that he would never set foot upon the field of battle; and it was by dint of these same connections and a talent for political infighting that he had risen to his position of eminence. But now he saw himself as a warrior, triumphant and painted with the blood of his enemies. And yet he was not, in this vision, intemperate. Oh, no. He would assure himself of the facts before acting. He would weigh his choices. Then and only then would....

✴

"Mister!"

A boy and a girl—both of junior-high age—were standing in front of Jimmy. The boy was skinny and rodentlike, had tipped hair and wore a white T-shirt with spattery red letters spelling out the words JESUS WHO? The girl, a strawberry blond of no appreciable beauty, was demurely dressed in jeans and a crewneck sweater. The cluttered noise of the crowd was that of a thousand people all saying the same thing slightly out of synch.

"You were talking weird shit in your sleep," said the boy, and the girl giggled.

Jimmy could not get the colonel out of his head. He stared at the boy with the ferocity of a man who has just received news that has left him in no mood to suffer fools. It seemed his eyes were boring like slow bullets into the boy's eyes.

"He's fucked up on something," the boy said in a hushed tone that put Jimmy in mind of a golf announcer explaining a difficult lie to the viewing audience. The girl leaned into him and took his hand: he was so wise.

Jimmy hefted the Colt, still warm from the telling, and laid it on the table. He got to his feet. Yawned.

"What kinda gun's that?" the girl asked. "Is it worth a lotta money?"

"Colt forty-five automatic, Model Nineteen-Eleven," Jimmy said. "Designed by John Browning. Damn near the same sidearm's been used by the U.S. Army these last ninety years. This one here's worth a good bit."

"He's just talking more shit," the boy said.

"You know where you are?" Jimmy asked him.

The boy affected a tone only slightly more doltish than his natural one. "Naw. Where am I?"

"That's my one rule of life," Jimmy told him. "Know where you are. You don't know that, you don't never see it coming."

The girl tugged anxiously at the boy, urging him away. "You fucking with us?" said the boy.

"Not yet...but I'm tempted."

In a cute show of defiance, the girl flipped him off and stuck out her tongue. Jimmy grinned, staggered back, pretending to be heart-shot. She giggled again. The boy, perhaps sensing a rival, slung an arm about her shoulder and steered her off toward safer ground.

Jimmy watched them join the sluggish flow of hunters, browsers, T-shirt collectors, and potential murderers milling about the aisles. Over by Doug Lindsay's table, a local TV crew had set up and under hot lights an enthusiastic brunette was, he assumed, saying something like, "...whether or not these particular guns should be banned from the marketplace continues to be a hot issue. But most of these folks have already made up their minds, and they're just out to have a good time. Back to you, Frank."

As Jimmy took a seat, a squat sixtyish man, bald except for a ruff of gray hair, carrying a Barney's Guns shopping bag, came up and pointed at the sign leaning on the display case. "That for real?" he asked. "Serious inquiries only?"

"It's what she says."

"Well, I got a serious inquiry." The man squared his shoulders and arranged his features into a sober mask and set himself as if he were about to lift an enormous weight. "What's it all about?" He stared deadpan at Jimmy for a beat, then laughed until his face grew red. "That serious enough for ya?"

Postal worker, Jimmy thought. Long divorced and given over to solitary drinking. Favorite TV show: *Cops*.

"What's it all about?" the man said again, and shook his head in glee.

Jimmy found that he was considering the question, though in terms the gray-haired man might have judged irrelevant. "I'll have to get back to you," he said.

✦

After her nap, Rita drove to a Buy-Rite for Alka Seltzer. She hung in the aisles, enjoying the antiseptic smell, picking up bottles of skin lotion and transistor radios and packets of pencils, not really interested in buying anything, just nosing around like a cat exploring unfamiliar territory. Her brain idled, releasing stray thoughts. A Muzak version of an old Stones song began to play. "Two Thousand Light Years from Home." Shoppers holding plastic baskets drifted past. She had been inside the store for two or three minutes when she noticed that a skinny young guy in a white shirt with Buy-Rite stitched in red on the pocket was following her. She ducked around a corner and hid behind a stand-up display of sunglasses. When the guy came up, she stepped out at him. "You're right," she said. "I'm here to rob your ass blind. I'm after Post-It Notes, legal pads, aspirin. Shit's worth a fortune on the street."

The guy adopted a wounded look. "Ma'am, I…"

"It's okay. I understand," Rita told him, and smiled. "From a distance you probably thought I was black."

"I'm just doing my job." The guy glanced toward the rear of the store—hoping for assistance, it seemed.

"Course you are. But now you see I'm a Native American, you realize I'm not after sundries, I'm after liquor." She glanced about inquiringly. "You do have a liquor department?"

"We got beer," the guy said uncertainly.

"Be vigilant," Rita said. "Don't confuse those stereotypes."

Once he was out of sight, she opened a box of Alka Seltzer and slipped the packets into her shirt pocket. She was heading for the exit when she spotted Loretta Snow browsing in an aisle devoted to health care products. Affecting the style of the guy in the Buy-Rite shirt, though more efficiently, Rita tracked her progress, watched her slip two bottles of children's vitamins, a couple of toothbrushes, a Pokemon action figure, and a motorcycle Barbie into her voluminous purse. That Ms. Snow was stealing for her kids spoke to Rita, who recalled having to go Christmas shoplifting for her own kids after her ex-husband had run off. Maybe, she thought, sweet little Loretta wasn't all weak tea and trembly chins. One thing for sure, she was no great shakes at petty theft. Before stuffing an item into the purse, she would lift her head and peer about the store, her hand poised above the thing desired, and after acquiring it, she would hurry away from the site of the theft, head down, clutching the purse to her chest, the picture of guilt. Assuming this was not her first such foray into crime, it was amazing that she had not been caught — to Rita's mind, Ms. Snow did not have the look of someone who had ever been caught.

As Ms. Snow turned into the candy aisle, hovering by a selection of imported chocolates, Rita spotted Mr. Buy-Rite homing in on her, moving stealthily along a cross-aisle. Rita quick-footed it down the aisle adjoining the one in which Ms. Snow was stationed. When she reached the cross-aisle she kicked the bottom of a stand supporting a pyramid of vacuum-packed cashews. The pyramid collapsed. Cans clattering, rolling in every direction. The sound alerted Ms. Snow. She gazed wildly about, then hustled toward the exit. The Buy-Rite guy stood glaring at Rita, hands on hips.

"Spill on Aisle Four," she said. "Sorry." She picked up one of the cans and inspected it. "Damn! This is cheap! I'm gonna get some of these for my husband."

She caught up with Ms. Snow in the parking lot — the woman was fumbling with the keys to an old Toyota wagon, its every ding and scar showing under the strong sunlight.

"Hey, Loretta!" Rita called.

Ms. Snow wore a hunted look, as if she were seeing not Rita, but some terrible and unfeeling authority.

"Don't worry," Rita said, coming up beside her. "You're in the clear. The junior G-man back there's too busy picking up his nuts to bother about you."

The woman's expression changed to one of perplexity. "Didn't you see him?" Rita leaned against a Ford SUV parked next to the Toyota. "Skinny little fart in a Buy-Rite shirt. He was coming to bust ya, honey. That's how come I knocked over the nuts."

Denial came and went in Ms. Snow's face. "I..." she said. "I don't..."

"Ain't no thing," Rita said. "I've stole for my kids. But if I was you, I wouldn't do no shopping here for a while. Fact is, you need to work on your technique before you go shopping anywhere." She tapped Ms. Snow's purse. "Don't make such a big production out of it. Just grab what you want...or maybe walk around with it, see who's watching before you stash it. Most of your store ferrets are looking for someone acts suspicious. You steal something right in front of them, they'll never notice. Like here..." Rita held out the can of cashews she had been hiding behind her. "Your kids like nuts?"

Seeming dazed, Ms. Snow nodded.

Rita handed her the can and pointed to a latte cart in front of a Safeway across the street. "Let's you and me get a cup of coffee. I'm paying."

They crossed the street, ordered an Americano (Rita) and a double tall latte (Ms. Snow), and stood in the sun beside the cart.

"Best thing to do," Rita said, "is just strip the packaging off and steal what's inside. That way, even if they stop you, they can't tell where the hell you got it."

Ms. Snow sipped, peered at her over the lid of her coffee.

"You ain't talking much," Rita said.

"I'm embarrassed. I don't usually...do anything like that."

"Things are bad, you do what you gotta." Rita set her coffee down on the edge of the cart. The barista, a good-looking guy with shoulder-length hair and a wispy mustache, flashed a smile, which she ignored. "You gonna be all right," she said to Ms. Snow. "You done well coming to Jimmy. He'll move that Colt for ya."

"I hope so."

"It's a done deal. He's already hooked a buyer."

"I know…he told me."

Rita shaded her eyes so she could watch a jet plane inching across the bright sky, about to vanish in the blaze of the sun. "I like you, Loretta. I didn't at first — " she turned back to Ms. Snow " — but I was in a bad mood. I wasn't looking at your situation. But knowing what you'd do for your kids, even if you don't do it so good…"

This elicited a nervous giggle from Ms. Snow.

"…that lets me see sharper. One thing I see bothers me, though. You're looking for a hero, Loretta, and I think you looking at Jimmy."

Ms. Snow's smile flattened out.

"I understand how it is," Rita went on. "There's been times I was looking for one myself. Son of a bitch never did show up."

Two pretty thirtyish women who had emerged from a hair salon in the mini-mall next to the Safeway approached the cart, and the barista fawned over them, calling them by name, asking how their day was going.

"I think you've got the wrong idea," Ms. Snow said with delicate firmness, as if she didn't want to offend, but felt compelled to make her position clear.

"Honey, I can see the way things are even if you can't. I got no problem with you. Could be Jimmy's the hero you been looking for. But he ain't *your* hero. Understand the difference?"

Ms. Snow put her coffee down beside Rita's. "I should go."

"Don't get your back up. I ain't telling you this 'cause I'm trying to stake out my territory. That's not my concern."

"Then why are you telling me?" Ms. Snow asked in a cool voice, an inch or two of steel showing above that soft white sheath.

"What you need to do," Rita said, "is let things play out with the Colt. Take your money and go to Seattle. Don't get in any deeper."

"It sounds," Ms. Snow said carefully, "like you're threatening me."

A black Firebird swerved out of a gas station down the street and burned rubber past the cart; a long-haired kid in the passenger seat stuck his head out the window and yelled some mad and mostly unintelligible business about pussy. Ms. Snow appeared rattled.

"I'm cautioning you," Rita said. "This ain't about me. It's about you. Jimmy's took with you some, and you're...vulnerable." She gave a snort of laughter. "I hate this Oprah Winfrey shit, but that's how it is. You're vulnerable, and the two of you might end up making the same mistake together. Now that'd piss me off, but I wouldn't lose my mind or nothing. All I'm saying is, maybe you oughta think about it. Y'know, if the subject comes up."

Ms. Snow thinned her lips, dabbed at them with a napkin. "I appreciate what you did over there." She gestured toward the Buy-Rite. "But I guess I don't understand exactly what you're saying."

"Don't go trying to figure it out." Rita told her. "You don't have enough information. Just take it to heart."

Ms. Snow squinted at Rita, as if she had suddenly gone out of focus. The barista asked if they wanted a refill, and Rita said, "No."

"I should go," Ms. Snow said again, but gave no sign of leaving; then: "Is everything all right? I mean with the gun?"

"I told ya, it's a done deal." Rita pointed to the purse. "I was you, I'd strip the packaging off the things you took before I went back to your car. Just in case."

The Firebird returned, pulled into the Safeway lot, stopped near the cart, its sunstruck body quivering like an overheated dog. The driver stuck his tongue out at them and waggled it around, while his passenger laughed to see such wit. Rita envied the boys. So full of dope and glory, the endless low-grade buzz of high school like a horizonless world they believed they could escape. Ms. Snow turned her back on the car and fiddled with the strap of her purse.

Twilight hung a dusty curtain over the town, the light gray like coffin lace wrapped around some old bride's bones. Jimmy followed the expressway up into the Cascades, humps of spruce and granite, the shape of country hams setting on their sliced sides. A milky green river meandered through the valley on his right. South and east, away from the mountains, the pale sky stretched on forever. He drove slowly, the radio tuned to crackly '80s rock and roll. An eighteen-wheeler passed him on the upgrade, taking so long to manage it, he had time to check the tread on its tires, read all the fine print on its rear doors. Cars whipped by as if coming from a universe where minutes had a quicker value.

He thought about the story, about what Rita had advised him after coming back from her nap. Make Susan stronger, she'd said. I can't give a damn about her 'less she shows some spirit. That seemed right, but he didn't want to make her too strong. Hell, he figured she'd had to be plenty strong as it was to survive being the prisoner in the colonel's one-person jail. He imagined her at the writing table in her bedroom, translating a poem Luis had written for her, armed with a Spanish-English dictionary. The lines she had just finished translating had caused her to fall into a daydream:

> …when I contemplate the idol of your sex,
> a little cat asleep in a silk basket, nested
> in the absolute acceptance of its self-embrace…

She was thinking about making love with Luis that morning, about the intensity of her physical reactions, considering clinically the specifics of those reactions. A few months previous, she would not have been able to entertain those thoughts — she had not known such thoughts existed. They were unladylike, occasionally causing her to flush, but she exulted in them, indulged in them, until those same reactions began to manifest anew. She recalled his face above hers in the yellow light of the early sun, mahogany carved in a mask of passionate exertion, his hair a black lava flow, and she recalled, too, how each movement of his body illuminated her with heat and pleasure. But she could not sustain memory against the depression that enclosed her as securely as the gates of the estate. Why, she asked herself, could she not move? When she focused her mental glass upon Luis, when she considered the virtues of the relationship, not merely the lovemaking but the world he offered, a world of mutual caring and adventurous interests, Havana at night and the beaches on the Isle of Pines, there seemed nothing she could refuse him. Yet when she turned her gaze the least bit to left or right, her vision of a life with him was shredded on the iron fences of restraint and restriction. Were those fences so unbreachable? Surely her father, were he to learn of her suffering, would not wish her to stay? He would find some way to avoid utter ruin. And Luis…She knew he would survive her husband's retribution. His spirit would never permit him to fail. Why, then, could she not move? Despairing of thought, recognizing it for another kind of prison, she rested her head on her arms, and remained that way for a long time, drifting in a quiet, desolate place where the only perturbation was the erratic humming of her mind. If she had someone to confide in, she told herself. Perhaps a more objective eye focused upon the subject would generate a flash of inspiration, an aperture through which she might see the possibility of hope.

The image of her cousin Aaron emerged, it seemed, from no particular thread of logic or filament of wish, simply appearing as if dredged by random process from the depths of remembrance. She had been able to talk to Aaron, but in the years immediately prior to her marriage, difficulties had arisen between them. Difficulties of a disturbing nature. His hand had come to linger on her arm, her back, and his kisses had grown less cousinly, until at last, while they were walking in the garden one evening, he had, in a manner touched both with apology and desperation, confessed his love to her. The shock of this confession left her stricken, and she had made him promise never to speak of this to her again. Her affection for him was so firmly seated, she had been consoling in her rejection; yet things had changed between them. He had relocated to New York City and sent a note on the occasion of her wedding saying that business prevented him from attending the ceremony.

Perhaps, she thought, the years had contrived a remedy for his misdirected ardor. And even if they had not, what did she risk by seeking him out? He could do no worse than reject her. Exhilarated by the prospect, by the hope—however slim—that something might be done, she removed a sheaf of linen paper from the desk drawer, chose a silver pen from among half a dozen in the holder, and began to write:

> My Dearest Cousin,
>
> It may seem strange that after so many years I am breaking the silence between us. Stranger yet that I am doing so without introductory pleasantry or preamble of any sort. But I am too impatient for such, and I hope that for the sake of our deep connection, you will set aside bitterness and any other emotion that may hamper an exchange of letters, for I have urgent need of your good will and concerned counsel...

It was dark by the time Jimmy turned onto the winding track that led up to Borchard's place. Potholes jolted the van, and he had to concentrate on holding the road. Swatches of a psychotic-looking landscape strobed in the headlights.

Clumsy dark green boughs swatted the windshield like bear-
ish arms and thumped on the roof. A glint of barbed wire
tangles, a heap of white sticks. A glittery gravel track littered
with empty shotgun casings. Pebbles rattled and cracked
against the suspension. Something with glowing amber eyes
scooted into the underbrush ahead. Grinding the gears, he
climbed past a caved-in shack, its door hanging one-hinged,
a rifle target tacked to a half-collapsed wall. He urged the
van up a final section of grade, then turned into a flat open
area rutted by tire tracks, lit by floods, bounded by a double-
gated entrance fashioned of planks and heavy-gauge wire.
He killed the ignition, jumped out and walked over to the
gate. Locked. Suspended above the gate was a signboard,
and painted on it was a design of a stag with red eyes rampant upon the American flag. The lights of a big house
showed through the trees.

"Hey!" he shouted. "Hey! Anybody up there?"

"Put your hands on your fucking head!" said a voice behind him.

Startled, Jimmy complied.

"Awright! Turn around!"

A pale compact man with a girlish mouth and brushcut
hair that looked white under the lights was training an M-16
at his chest. "I don't know you," he said.

"I come to see Ray Borch…"

The man snapped, "I ask who you come to see?"

"You didn't ask nothing," said Jimmy calmly. "All you
said was you didn't know me."

"I love it when a wiseass comes walking in my woods."
The man shifted closer — pale eyebrows gave his face a rudi-
mentary, posthuman look. "Keep it up, okay?"

"I come to see Ray Borchard about maybe selling him a
gun."

"He's getting ready for a meeting. Man's got enough
guns, he don't need yours." The man made a flicking gesture with the rifle. "You trespassing, y'know that?"

"He sure acts like he needs this gun," Jimmy said. "Offered me six thousand for it."

The man's blue-eyed squint seemed to be inspecting him for flaws. "You the one holding Bob Champion's Colt?"

"Sure am."

Disappointment in his voice, the man said, "Awright, come on. I'll walk you up."

At the end of a steep and crooked path lay a ramshackle hunting lodge, two stories of split logs with a screen porch, bounded by secondary-growth spruce, chokecherry bushes close by the steps. Old filmy, flyless spiderwebs tented the leaf tops. The white-haired man parted with Jimmy inside the door and went upstairs to fetch the major, leaving him in a room as big as a lobby, furnished with groupings of brown leather chairs and brass lamps with Tiffany shades and crocheted throw rugs. Jimmy took a stroll around. Mounted on the walls were imitation Currier and Ives prints and display cabinets containing dozens of guns, including a fancy dueling pistol of eighteenth century design that snagged his interest until he identified it as a copy. Brass ashtrays on the end tables. The back wall was dominated by a fireplace you could have parked a Volkswagen in. A crackling blaze gave off a blood-orange radiance and a spicy smell of burning spruce. Jimmy dropped into a chair to one side. Above the mantel hung a framed photograph of five men in tiger fatigues standing on a dusty plain. Its surface was glazed with reflection, and he couldn't tell if Borchard was among the men, though he supposed he would be. He didn't much care for the room. It looked like set decoration, your basic split-rail Hollywood rustic getaway, and not a place that bespoke the personality of its owner. There sure as hell was nothing that brought Bob Champion and his sorry life to mind.

He started thinking about his story again. Susan at her writing desk, several weeks after the previous scene, translating another of Luis' poems:

I am no longer content to be a tragic figure
in your sky, an imaginary valentine,
ten memories in a manila folder,
or a handful of dry poetry —
for there is between us more
than all these maudlin trinkets signify.
Matters that require majesties of resolution,
energy that demands expression,
gold tides of it, evangels of an important glory…

It was a brave statement. Demanding. She could not fault him for being so. God knows, she deserved worse for all she had caused him to endure. Each time she reread the poem, she was forced to consider breaking things off, but she knew that were she to bring the subject up, all his bravery — and hers — would go glimmering. With a sigh, she returned to the last stanza, upon which she was currently working:

…the first preconscious glimmer
that started up the Beast from hibernation,
and goaded it with the memory of your skin
beneath its shaping hands,
and so encouraged it to draft an obsessed design
of death and people, claws and stings,
that provided me these words of doubtful worth
with which to sing and charm you,
and set a stag with ruby eyes
to guard the treasure of your birth…

She didn't like the word "provided," but "gave" was too plain and "sent" untrue to the meaning. "Impart?" No. Perhaps, she thought, she should change the entire construction and that would permit her to find a better choice. A knock at the door jarred her. The maid stuck her head in and said, "*Señora, un carta para usted.*"

"*Pase!*" Susan said.

The maid brought her the letter, then, with a curtsey, left the room and softly closed the door.

Lucius Shepard

When she saw her cousin's name on the envelope, Susan's heart leapt. She opened it hurriedly:

Dearest Susan,

I must confess that my initial reaction upon reading your letter embodied all those harsh emotions that you have asked me to put aside. You must understand that while I cannot forgive myself for my regrettable actions that long-ago evening in my uncle's garden, or for having nurtured the feelings that provoked those actions, neither have I been able to forgive you for rejecting me. I'm certain this will make no sense to you. It makes none to me. Your reception of my overtures was far more kindly than I deserved. Nonetheless, I seem for the moment incapable of completely purging myself of anger and disappointment. Does this mean that I continue to harbor some shred of the inappropriate desire I once felt toward you? Perhaps so. And this being the case, I wonder if it is such a good idea for you to confide in me. However, when I recall the closeness of our relationship prior to that evening, the confidences we exchanged, the laughter we shared, and further, when I consider how I have missed talking to you these past years, I find I have no will to deny you my full attention and a friendly ear.

That said, I can only view the intimate details related in your letter with horror and outrage. Why you have kept the fact of your husband's degrading treatment of you from your family, I cannot guess. But now that you have revealed this sordid secret, I have not the least hesitation in advising you to do that which you say you cannot: you must leave Rutherford. Do you think that your father, for all his significant failings, would urge you to do otherwise? I assure you that he would not. Nor would any of us who love you want or expect you to continue in this depraved mockery of a marriage...

A tromping noise broke Jimmy's concentration. Major Raymond Borchard, outfitted in fatigue trousers, jacket, and infantry boots, was descending the stair, followed by the white-haired man.

"Mr. Guy!" Borchard's smile was so expansive, Jimmy figured if he kept it up, the corners of his lips might wind up meeting behind his head. "I'm told you had a change of heart about the Colt."

"You might say."

The white-haired man posted at the foot of the stair. Borchard crossed toward the fireplace. "Six thousand, then?"

"Hold on," Jimmy said. "We got us some talking to do."

Borchard's smile lost wattage; he took a parade rest stance and folded his arms. "About what?"

"About Susan, for one thing."

"Susan?" Borchard chewed on the name a second. "You can't be referring to my ex-wife's sister? She's the only Susan I know."

"What about ol' Susie Corliss?" asked the white-haired man. "Y'know, Mike Corliss' wife?"

"Sorry...my mind was drifting," said Jimmy, making a gesture that mimed erasure. "Loretta Snow's who I wanna talk about."

Borchard absorbed this. "Randy," he said to the white-haired man. "You'd better go down to the gate. The boys will be arriving soon."

Randy beat a sullen retreat, like a dog yelled at for barking, leaving the front door ajar, and Borchard settled in the chair opposite Jimmy's. He arranged his features into those of a forbidding judge with a comical mustache. "Proceed."

"Okay. Here's the deal." Jimmy leaned forward and rested his elbows on the arms of the chair. "I'm going let you bid on the Colt, but I got a condition."

"Wait a second," Borchard said coldly. "Bid?"

"That's right. I got another interested party. Only fair thing is to let you two bid it up."

"I made you an offer."

"Did I accept it?"

"No, but I thought I made myself clear."

"Ditto," said Jimmy. "Thing is, I come to change my mind. I'm a businessman. I need to move that Colt. But I ain't about to give it over 'cause you say so. You wanna hold it in your hot little hand, you can just bid on it."

Borchard stared at Jimmy. The snapping of the fire seemed to register the percussion of his angry thoughts. "Who will I be bidding against?" he asked.

Jimmy gave a wry chuckle. "Well, I ain't going tell you who. You might start intimidating him the way you tried to do me and Rita."

"Then how will I know the bidding is fair? Or that you even have another buyer?"

"'Cause that's how I do business. Fair. You ask around about me if you want."

"I know your reputation," Borchard said after a few more snaps. A log rolled over in the fireplace, sparks showered, the flames licked higher. "This condition you mentioned...?"

"I want you to keep away from Loretta Snow till the money's changed hands."

Borchard nodded, as if in response to an inner voice. "What has she told you about me?"

"That's between me and her."

"All right. Then tell me what your interest is in Loretta. Or is that between you and her as well?"

"I'd like to see the lady catch a break is all."

"Very high-minded," Borchard said. "You'll pardon me if I don't accept it as being completely forthcoming."

The man's pomposity was putting an edge on Jimmy. "I don't give a damn what you accept! That's what I'm telling ya."

Borchard let out a sigh that seemed to express a sadness arising from the foolishness with which he was being confronted. "You don't know Loretta, Mr. Guy. She's not as innocent as she pretends, and her connection to reality is at best tenuous. She plays the victim in a story she likes to tell herself about her life. She may be borderline psychotic."

Jimmy's face grew warm, and in his mind he felt anger slide forward, like a beast sneaking on its belly close to something tasty. He shook a forefinger at the major for emphasis as he spoke. "See, that's another thing I don't give a damn about. What you got to say about her and what she got to say about you. Just you keep away from her, and we'll get this done. But I hear about any trouble, I'm cutting you out, and that's a fact." He folded the finger into his fist, tapped the knuckle against his jaw. "We good?"

Jimmy could hear voices coming through the open front door. Five or six men walking up the path, it sounded like.

"I think we can do business," Borchard said, getting to his feet smartly; he beckoned to Jimmy. "Why don't we take this out back."

He guided Jimmy along a dimly lit corridor, through a screen door, down some steps, and out into a grassy, well-lit space that had been fixed up into a shooting range. Four pistols, a pair of binoculars, and an auto-loader lay on a crudely carpentered stand behind which shooters would position themselves. Targets were bull's-eyes affixed to a backing of sandbags at the far end. The reek of cordite mixed in with the scent of sweet resins. A thin crescent moon made glowing smoke of the treetop mist. Dark evergreens stood grave and winded all around, as if in judgment over the place.

"I'd like you to understand why I want the Colt so badly," said Borchard as they approached the stand. "Do you know much about Bob Champion?"

"Ain't important what I know," Jimmy said. "You the one's got the urge to explain himself."

The major folded his arms, lifted his eyes, as if contemplating a distant source of light. "Champion was a racist in the beginning, it's true. But unlike others of his stamp, he outgrew his beginnings and came to recognize that racism was simply a perversion of a greater struggle — the struggle to protect individual liberties. He was not an educated man, yet his writings display an eloquent sense of the core meaning of justice. He took up arms in the hope of drawing attention to the principles involved."

"Uh-huh," said Jimmy, running a finger along the trigger guard of a Glock .357 that was resting on the stand.

"He was carrying the Colt when he died," the major went on. "His ammunition was gone except for a single round chambered in the Colt. He might have killed one of his assailants with that bullet, but I believe he knew what a powerful symbol the gun and its one remaining bullet might someday prove to be. He hid it in the house, where only Loretta was likely to find it, then walked out into the fire of the F.B.I. This — " he fumbled in his pocket, extracted a ring box, and opened it to reveal a brass-cased bullet resting on red velvet " — this is the bullet. Loretta gave it to me during better days."

Repressing a smile, Jimmy pretended to examine the Glock.

"I intend to marry this bullet to the Colt once again," the major said, using a sonorous tone such as a preacher might use to announce his decision to harrow a demon from a possessed child. "I intend to bring Bob Champion's spirit to the world."

"Speaking of Ms. Snow telling stories," Jimmy said, "appears you got a pretty good fairy tale going yourself. Bob Champion died alone. Least that's what Rita says. For all you know, he mighta gone out pissing hisself and squalling like a baby."

"Then why hide the gun?"

"Hell, I don't know…and you don't, either. Maybe he'd lost his mind. Thing I can't figure is whether you come to believe your own bullshit, or if you just jerking off till you can scoop up a better grade. Y'know, one'll have more mass appeal."

"Have you read any of Champion's writing? Or is that just a knee-jerk reaction?"

"Never read the writing on a roll of toilet paper, but I know it'll wipe my ass."

Before the major could respond, Jimmy said, "Look here, man. I don't care if Bob Champion wrote the goddamn Magna Carta. I sell guns. That's what I care about."

"You're not concerned that an American hero, a martyr who laid down his life…"

"Hero?" Jimmy held the Glock barrel-up. "Any loser can play hero with one of these. If Champion was such a hero, how come his wife was wanting to run away all those years?"

Laughter issued from the house. The major hearkened to it, then turned back to Jimmy. "Is that what Loretta said? I'm afraid she's misled you again, Mr. Guy."

"Now, y'see…this is where we're getting into that area I don't wanna hear about."

"What would you like to hear? Apparently I need guidelines if we're to have a conversation."

"I got something you can tell me." Jimmy sucked on his teeth, made them squeak. "You think you talk at me long enough, this ray of light's gonna come shining into my brain, and I'm going to kneel down and offer you the Colt on a pillow? Maybe one matches the color of that pretty little ring box?"

Major Borchard gave out with a tired noise. He indicated the Glock. "Care to try your hand?" he asked.

Jimmy shrugged, said, "Sure." He hefted the gun, checked to see if there was one in the pipe. He took the stance, sighted, then pulled off four rounds. The detonations seemed to stir a little extra sighing from the surrounding trees. Borchard peered at the grouping through the binoculars. "Not too bad," he said.

"Pretty damn good considering the junk I was shooting with." Jimmy eyed Borchard expectantly.

"You didn't finish the clip," Borchard said.

There was a slyness to the words that rankled Jimmy. He laid the Glock down. "I keep getting this feelin'," he said, "you think you can play me. Drag me into some kinda mind game."

"Maybe you're paranoid." Borchard picked up a revolver from the end of the counter. "Happens all the time."

"Jesus!" Frustrated, Jimmy punched at the stand. "What? You gonna show me how good you shoot, now? Threaten me? You ain't hearin' me, man. You can't fuck with my head. Either I'm too damn stupid, or else you just ain't that slick. About a minute, I'm hopping in my van and heading east. So you got anything more to say relates to business, you best spit it out."

After a silence Borchard set down the revolver. "I want the bids in writing...and notarized."

"I can get them faxed," said Jimmy. "Maybe my bidder'll take the time to get 'em notarized. But I ain't going to hold him to it, he doesn't want to. You wanna see them right when they come, I'll call you and you can pick them up yourself."

Reluctantly, Borchard said, "Agreed."

"Well, I believe that about takes care of things, then." Jimmy pointed off to the side of the lodge. "Can I get to the path through there? Wouldn't wanna disrupt your meeting."

"You're welcome to attend."

"Naw...Y'know how it is. I gotta go polish my tooth-brush."

"I understand," Borchard said smoothly, coldly. "You can only put some things off for so long."

Jimmy threaded his way through bushes to the front of the lodge, stopped to brush off flecks of leaf that had caught on his shirt and trousers. Despite his ridicule of Borchard, he'd had a whistling-past-the-graveyard type of feeling when he turned his back on the man, and he wasn't easy with being alone in the middle of the White Paradise with disciples inside ready to heed their master's call. As he started down the path, passing beyond the light shining from the windows, into the shadow of the old-growth spruce, he heard the major shout, "What is the name?"

"Bob Champion!" answered a ragged chorus.

"Who is the enemy?" shouted the major.

A long gust of wind shook loose a groaning vowel from the assembly of boughs, outvoicing the response; a night bird sounded a loopy, flutelike cry, and visible through a cut in the treeline, the sickle moon sailed free of the mist and stood on its point directly between two mountains in the west.

To honor the sabbath, the gun show did not open its doors until noon on Sunday. Rita and Jimmy stayed in bed late, watching HBO, breakfasting on cold pizza and diet Sprites from the vending machine next to the office. The carpet strewn with crumpled cans, clothing, take-out cartons, receipt books, magazines, candy wrappers, sections of newspaper that had been stepped on by shower-wet feet and gotten stuck and had to be kicked off. Rita had removed a dresser drawer, placed it by the bed, and was using it to hold a bag of ice. Potato chips floated in the melt at the bottom of the drawer.

They were watching a movie called the *The Education of Little Tree*. The *TV Guide* billed it as "an evocative tale of an eight-year-old Cherokee orphan who has come to live with his Native American grandmother and white grandfather." Rita thought it was for shit. The Cherokee orphan was played by an Indian boy who resembled a cute white kid, and the grandmother was the stereotypical wise old woman in touch with the nature of corn and the Buffalo Spirit—a repository for the secret wisdom of an ancient race. When she used traditional herbs to draw rattlesnake poison from her husband's hand, which was swollen up like a Mickey Mouse hand, and started talking to the cute kid about his warrior heritage, Rita lost patience.

Lucius Shepard

"See if something else is on," she said to Jimmy, who had gained possession of the remote.

"Ain't nothing else but preachers and infomercials," he said grumpily.

"Try the preachers. They're funny sometimes."

"How come you never complain when it's some dumbass movie about white people?"

"This *is* about white people, Jimmy."

"It's got Graham Green in it. You like Graham Green."

"Gimme the damn remote!" She reached beneath the covers, hand-fought him for control. Her fingers brushed his dick, felt it twitch. She fisted it, squeezed. "Give it to me."

He grinned. "Keep that up, I'll give you something."

She loosened her grasp, stroked him gently. When he was ready, she came astride his hips and fitted him to her. With her knees high, she sank down, slid forward, rocked up, then sank down again…a luxuriant rhythm that triggered a jab of pleasure with each repetition. Her thoughts circled with the languid regularity of her movements, passing from momentary observation to momentary oblivion and back. The way he looked. Sleepy but rapt. Like a boy doing his best to stay awake to watch the end of his favorite show. His fingers gouged her ass, pulling her down harder, sending a hot charge into her belly. She grabbed the headboard, kept it from banging the wall, and let him guide her. Behind her shut-tight lids, a thin strip of light traced a curved horizon, the sun in eclipse. Something shifted inside her, a switch clicked, a relay engaged, something…and a passway opened, allowing the charge in her belly to spread throughout and build into a wave. Distantly, she heard the chuffing of Jimmy's breath and herself saying love words. She tossed back her head and caught a glimpse of gray Sunday through the cracked drapes. The wave was still inside her, but it had grown taller than her, wider, as if the real Rita was a tiny creature living deep in her flesh, in the shadow of the wave, and when it broke she seemed to be lifted and tumbled and almost killed. All but a flicker of her flame extinguished.

72

Waking to the world again, she felt ungainly, out of her medium, a beached mermaid straddling a man who pumped furiously into her, his head raised, face flushed, going at it like a cocaine monkey. She rolled her hips to bring him off. His fingers hooked her waist, grinding her against him until he went rigid and said, "Oh, shit...Jesus!" She unstuck strands of hair from her sweaty face, worked her hips some more as he softened, then collapsed half-atop him. He made a contented noise in his throat, ran a hand along her flank.

"Can I have the remote now?" she asked.

"I love you," he said groggily.

The words made her heart fail, so it had to jump back into rhythm. Whenever that happened, she always wondered if it was love or some associated terror that caused it.

"I love you," she said, kissed him, and searched around under the covers for the remote, found it down beside his knee.

He closed his eyes, breathed deeply. "Don't put on no preacher, okay?"

She sat up in bed, channel-surfed until she hit a Bugs Bunny cartoon. Bugs was on the battlement of a frontier fort, firing a cannon at Yosemite Sam. She watched a few minutes, then took to surfing again. Channel 13 was showing an X-Files episode, but it was almost over. Jimmy murmured something, then he said, "Aaron..."

She cut the sound on the TV so she could hear. "What's that?"

"I have to write Susan," he said.

"Jimmy, you awake?"

He didn't answer at first. Finally he said, "Naw...not really."

"Who's Aaron?"

He blinked at her. "The hero."

"In your story? You didn't tell me about him."

"Later," he said. "Okay?"

She gave his shoulder a shake. "C'mon, Jimmy! Don't hold out on me!"

Lucius Shepard

He licked his lips, blinked, and wiped his mouth with the back of a hand. Sleepily, speaking in phrases at first, but then with greater energy, curving the sentences into fancy shapes, he told her a little about Aaron, then returned to an earlier portion of the narrative that concerned Susan's intensifiying involvement with Luis and her increasing frustration with the colonel. Rita thought how strange it was that Jimmy's daddy had been able to pound dents into his brain in just such a way so as to cause him to go groping around in life most of the time—business-sharp, but otherwise dim as a firefly, except when it came to making his stories. They arose from a place inside him she couldn't see or touch, and it was this mystery, she believed, its resonance with her and not the stories themselves, that inspired the parts she sometimes played and let her become her own incarnation, a story unto herself. She pictured a waterfall in his head, splashing down onto rocks amid a pine forest, amazing creatures materializing from the roiled-up water and vanishing, silver wolves and cavemen and private eyes and flashily dressed women...and she felt the story of Colonel Rutherford's Colt charging a battery inside her, sending forth a voltage that was disintegrating the drab curtain of ordinary concerns that muffled her spirit, liberating it to act. She had a premonition that this story might take them both right to the edge.

Jimmy's voice trailed off and he turned his head away. His breathing grew slow and regular. Rita watched a commercial for an Internet service that featured groups of shiny young folk, one of every race except her own, all made ecstatic by their access to endless quantities of porn and merchandise. Then she settled on her side next to Jimmy. His eyelids were fluttery with dreams. She touched her lips to his cheek, and he whispered too low to hear. Probably dreaming about the story. Often when he fucked her she wasn't sure whether he'd gotten lost in a story and was doing someone named Charlotte or Marie...or Susan. She wondered what it was like, having stories in your head. It was hard enough pretending to be yourself, sifting through all the garbage floating in your mind and finding the thoughts that mattered, that streamed up pure from the place you streamed up from. She leaned over him, kissed his mouth. Inhaled his sweet warm smell. An easy stirring in her gut caused her to think about waking him. She recalled a time in Oregon City when she climbed on board the Jimmy train an hour before opening and hadn't jumped off until half past six. She just couldn't get enough of the crazy bastard. And when he was working on a story, he couldn't get enough of her. Like his dick was connected to the part of his brain did the telling. It would be fun, she thought. If the Colt was going to sell, they didn't need a good day. But she let the notion slide. She dug the remote from a fold in the blanket, aimed it at the TV, and changed channels.

Sunday afternoon was slow for everyone. The big spenders generally waited until the last day to buy, and most of the sensible shoppers had come and gone, leaving gawkers and curiosity seekers and shoplifters to turtle along the aisles, causing the dealers to view with suspicion every roomy jacket and purse. No one ever tried to steal from the Guy Guns tables, because the weapons were under lock and key; but Rita liked spying out shoplifters at the adjacent tables, so Jimmy let her handle the business and sat off to the side of things. Most times he enjoyed doing the shows, but today it unnerved him. Lights were too harsh, chatter troubled his ears. And the smell…It was as if cleaning agents and neat's-foot oil and people and freshly dried T-shirts and corn dogs and everything else had canceled each other out, and what remained was a faint oily residue of deadness left by the passage of thousands of rounds through the barrel of an enormous gun.

He tried to climb back into his story, but couldn't find an opening. A sun-drenched linoleum floor sprang to mind. Dirty; with pieces of lettuce mired in a gravy film; the whole thing iridescent with grease. Under the scum lay a pattern of weird abstract shapes. Once when he was fifteen he'd dropped some acid and spent all day tracing the shapes on flimsy, opaque paper. Cowboys, Indians, devils hiding in clouds, winged monsters — dozens of images surfacing from the family filth as if he had unearthed their true genealogy, their spiritual history. The sheets of paper adhered to the floor, ripping when he tried to peel them off. A total mess. He didn't feel like cleaning it, so he went out to the barn and sat watching swallows fall like tiny desperate angels born from the holy radiance pouring through a loft window, their flurried wingbeats chasing the stillness. Whitish gold bars of light crumbled between long gaps in the boards. You could see anything within them. You could almost go inside them, visit the incandescent country they bordered. Moldy hay and ripe horseshit thick in his nostrils. The little stallion whuffling in his stall below. Hours like that. The light gapping the boards burned orange. The swallows nested. Then he heard his father scream his name. Nobody screamed like his old man. "Jimmaaaaay!" Spoken that way, it had the weight of a deadly Arabic curse, a word that meant "kill" or "die." It hadn't scared him that day. It seemed part of nature. An eagle sighting its violated nest would sound so. Such strength and fury, its red-hot edge had sliced a smile onto his face...

Rita was talking to a customer, a shrunken old man sporting a VFW pin on his baggy sports jacket. She stood one-footed, her left knee on a folding chair. Her ass shifted when she gestured, jeans clinging to every curve, and that got him remembering the morning. Who'd think you could fit so much meanness and so much sweetness into the same woman? She'd snap your dick off with a stare, then go soft and take your breath away. Between those contrary states, her arrow usually swung into the mean, but that was just her survival posture. Didn't bother him any. The old man wobbled off and she caught Jimmy staring. She tried to hide a smile, lost the battle, and sat down. She glanced over her shoulder at him, still smiling, her hair flipping away from her face—he saw her younger, how she must have looked before bad love walked in and money luck ran out. She didn't let that pretty girl loose too often. Jimmy remembered the days when she hadn't ever let her loose. She'd glared at everyone with hateful intensity. Their first conversation, she was working this armpit club in Billings on a slow Wednesday night, sitting on a barstool in a tight one-piece black dress that showed her off legs, tits, and shoulders. She'd priced herself at two hundred dollars. He said he didn't have that much, but he would tell her a story. A real story, not some bullshit. A genuine just-for-her work of the imagination. Whatever kind she wanted. A unique creation with hearts and lives on the line.

"What do I have to do?" she asked.

"Stick around for the telling is all," he replied. "Sometimes it takes a while."

He kicked out his legs, crossed them at the ankles. Still thinking about Rita, he relaxed, checked out the passing parade. He idly followed the progress of a skinny black guy who must have gone six-ten easy, heavy on the jewelry, expensively dressed. Jimmy was wondering if the guy might be one of the Sonics, when the image of the sabal palm flew into his mind, and along with it, like a shadow on the sun, Colonel Rutherford's bland, meticulous personality. He had arrived home after midnight, without announcing his presence to Susan, and now at nearly five in the morning—dressed in trousers, undershirt, and braces—was sitting in a wooden chair that he had set beneath the stairway in the corridor leading to Mariana's quarters (he had sent the housekeeper off to pass the evening with her sister in Varadero Beach). Now and then he leaned forward and looked off along the corridor and out the open door toward the little palm tree, isolated against the dark green backdrop of the grounds. He was nervous, his palms clammy, his respiration shallow and uneven. He anticipated no logistical difficulties, but he had never before killed a man, and the concept of such an act excited and alarmed him. The colonel's aversion to violence, even violence of the staged variety such as fencing and boxing contests, had become something of a joke amongst his fellow cadets at the Academy, and had ensured him a career spent behind a desk. Yet in this instance, violence was the sole remedy that would secure a proper resolution and the respect of his brother officers. Though he remained confident that he would carry through with his intention, and that he would suffer no reprisals, official or otherwise, for having shot an intruder, he was concerned about the possible psychological consequences—he had known soldiers who, albeit justified in their actions, had been afflicted by severe mental trauma. The idea that Carrasquel might haunt him in death was intolerable. The man had violated his marriage and thus forfeited humane consideration. He deserved not merely to die, but to be erased from memory, consigned to oblivion. These stern thoughts heartened the colonel and convinced him both of his moral right and of the shield that righteousness would contrive against self-recrimination. When he confronted Carrasquel, he would not see a man, but a vile error, and he would expunge it.

Five-thirty arrived and Carrasquel did not appear. Birds twittered in the crown of the ceiba tree, and a cart passed on the street beyond the wall, its wheels racketing. The colonel stationed himself just inside the door, afire with frustration. At first he blamed the quality of his information. Perhaps Doctor Lens had misled him as to the regularity of Carrasquel's entrances and exits. He admonished himself for not having brought his own investigation to bear. Then he realized that Susan and her lover might be so wholeheartedly engaged, they had lost track of time. He was tempted to creep up the stairs to Susan's chambers and burst in upon them, but decided he did not want to catch them at their passion. His imagination required no support in picturing their involvement. The original plan was best. He would wait.

The sun climbed higher, and the sapling palm was suffused in warm yellow light, seeming emblematic in its glowing solitude, as if it foreshadowed a holy imminence and

Colonel Rutherford's Colt

were itself a point above which the Virgin might momentarily appear to tender sweet cautions to the world, or even Christ himself manifest in all his bloody glory, his wounds still yielding crimson droplets that fell upon the ground to fertilize with sacred life the tree where he had come to teach some material perfection. This sight and his interpretation of it reinvigorated the colonel's less-than-holy purpose and restored to him the force of emotion he had experienced upon learning of his wife's infidelity. His frustration swelled into a petulant fury that in turn elevated him to a reach from which he believed he could distinguish the entire field of possibility, and from that height he could find no impediment to his craving for vengeance. No, not vengeance, he thought. Balance. That was what he most craved. An evening out of things, the employment of counterweights to preserve a workable if not desirable level of engagement. He studied the Colt in his hand, perceiving it to be the instrument of unqualified conviction. Its cold weight satisfied. The slotted shells, silent yet about to speak. He firmed his grip, caressed the trigger with the ball of his forefinger, and grew calm.

At four minutes past six by the colonel's watch, he heard the voices of a man and a woman issuing from above, pitched low and urgent. Then the closing of a window and muted noises of exertion, a foot scraping against the wall. Steeling himself, the colonel stepped out into the light of day. Carrasquel, wearing a striped dress shirt and coffee-colored slacks, tie and jacket draped over one arm, was suspended six feet above and to the left, clutching the vines that straggled across the yellow stucco wall. When he saw the colonel he froze like a lizard on a twig, his features aghast.

"Come down," said the colonel, backing away so as to prevent Carrasquel from leaping on him. He had, during the days preceding, prepared several versions of a speech, a recitation testifying to his disgust with the lovers and presenting his views on the finality of death. But seeing Carrasquel knocked all that from mind. His brain seemed to have be-

79

come a solid block of implacable hatred. "Come down" was all he could muster.

Once on the ground, his tie and jacket abandoned, Carrasquel said, "Colonel, listen to me," and held his hands palms up as though about to present a defense.

Colonel Rutherford put a finger to his lips and then pointed to Susan's window. Carrasquel must have perceived this signal to offer some hopeful possibility, for he nodded vigorously in assent and made a placatory gesture—he wanted to cooperate, to get past this moment. The colonel gathered himself, drew in a breath of the fresh morning air, and with all his might he shouted: "Susaaaaan!" Birds started up from the ceiba. Scant seconds later the bedroom window was flung open, and Susan leaned forth, her black hair disheveled, holding a filmy robe shut at her breasts. It was apparent that for an instant she did not fully comprehend the situation, but then terror washed the confounded expression from her face and she cried, "Oh, God! Please…Hawes!"

Faint hope had been replaced by resignation in Carrasquel's face. He looked up to the window, to Susan, and Colonel Rutherford thought he could actually make out the transit of emotion between them, a transparent tunnel created by their fused stares, along which a faint rippling, as of heat haze, was passing. They might not have known he was there. This disrespect, this fundamental neglect, so enraged the colonel, he pushed aside the doubts that had been nibbling at his determination. He aimed the Colt, locked his elbow, sighted, all with an easy fluidity and precision, and shot Luis Carrasquel in the head, and—as he pitched sideways, half-turning in his fall—in the side just below the pit of the arm.

Susan screamed her lover's name, then screamed again, an inarticulate cry to heaven, and began to sob, to speak brokenly—whether outpourings of grief or hatred, the colonel could not tell. He refused to look at her. The shots had caused his heart to race, but it was slowing now. He felt considerably less satisfaction than he might have expected, but that did not dismay him—emotional satisfaction had not been his goal. He considered the body, the sprays and poolings of blood, making certain that the physical details had no substantial power over him. The second bullet had spun Carrasquel so that he had toppled onto his belly, with his face partly buried in the grass. The initial entry wound was obscured, but from his vantage the colonel saw that a sizeable portion of skull had been removed from the back of the man's head. Gore clotted the hair surrounding the cavity. He had an annoying sense of the pulse in his neck and felt no little revulsion at the profusion of insect life already scurrying to welcome Carrasquel into the lower orders of the food chain. But nothing, in his view, that presaged the abnormal or the untoward.

It had not occurred to Colonel Rutherford to worry overmuch about Susan's reaction to the murder. He knew that she would do nothing. For the next nine days she did not leave her rooms. Each morning the colonel asked her maid to inquire after Susan's health. Only once did she respond, and then to ask permission to attend the funeral, a request he declined to honor. On the tenth morning, as he cast about for his briefcase in the alcove, she came down the stairs and addressed him in an exhausted voice. She wore a riding skirt and a gray blouse that had been misbuttoned. Her face was tear-stained, haggard, and she leaned on the banister with both hands, as if her legs could not support her. "I'm going to leave you," she said.

The colonel spotted his briefcase, snapped it open to ascertain whether it contained certain papers. He glanced at Susan, stepped to the door, threw it open and said, "Leave."

"I want your promise—" her voice caught "—that you won't harm my family."

"Unlike you," said the colonel, "I refrain from making promises I have no intention of keeping."

Susan feebly brushed hair back from her face. "You bastard!"

"Revile me if you wish," he said. "But it was not I who violated my vows. It was not I who brought my lover into the marriage bed."

"I had no choice! You never let me out of the house without one of your spies for company!"

"I see. If I had been less concerned for your safety, you would have slept with him in the...."

"Anywhere!" Susan descended a few steps, her face cinched with anger. "In the streets, the gutters....Anywhere! When I was with him, nothing else existed. And that was such a blessing!" Her anger peaking, she hissed the word "blessing" and came down yet another step. "Do you know why? Because when I was with him, there was no you!"

The colonel was taken aback. He had not realized Susan was capable of such strong emotion. The task ahead might well be more difficult than he had presumed.

"If you force...." A sob bubbled forth, and Susan's mouth worked. Then she continued in the tight, hushed voice of someone near to breaking. "If you force me to stay, I'll kill you!"

The colonel met her gaze with studied indifference. "Should you care to dine tonight," he said, "Porfirio will be doing his chicken." As a final insult, one he was certain she would understand, he left the door open behind him.

Of all the problems facing the colonel as a result of the murder, the most pressing was that posed by General Ruelas. He had known from the outset that were he to rid the world of Carrasquel, an affair between Susan and the general's nephew would be suspected, and this would shed a wan light on his motives for the shooting. People would say—as, indeed, they were saying—why, if not for love, would a young man of so much promise attempt to climb to the bedroom of a beautiful married woman? In his grief, General Ruelas might very well be persuaded by this point of view. The colonel understood that he needed to confront the general quickly. To this end, using as an excuse a land dispute involving the United States government and a group of Cuban citizens from the general's home province, he invited Ruelas to lunch at a Havana restaurant popular among the wealthy and powerful, a place of linen tablecloths and icy chandeliers where he and Ruelas would command an attentive audience. The more public their conversation, the better it would assist the colonel's design.

The general was a fit sixtyish man of diminutive stature who looked more at ease in a business suit than the comic opera uniform he wore at state functions. He had a closely trimmed gray goatee, thinning hair, and a bony, birdlike face. Not a menacing figure, yet he had a reputation for relentlessness both in war and in the political arena, and — if one were to believe the rumors — had no qualms concerning torture. This day he sported a black armband and was accompanied by a portly aide, also dressed civilian-style. Colonel Rutherford had previously sent a written apology to the Ruelas family, but once the general had seated himself and finished obsessively arranging his silverware into perfectly ordered ranks on the linen, the colonel again offered an apology, saying that if he had only recognized Luis, he would never have fired. All he had seen in the half-light had been a stranger attempting to break into his house.

The general inclined his head in what the colonel interpreted as an acknowledgment, but not an acceptance, and said, "Why do you think my nephew was at your house?" He kept his gaze focused on his aide's salad fork, as if coveting it for his little silver troop.

"I have no comprehension of your nephew's motives," said the colonel. "But I assure you, I have utter confidence in my wife's."

"My Dolores has not seen your wife at the Palace of late," the general said. "Is she ill?"

Lucius Shepard

Though nearly full, the restaurant had grown quiet since General Ruelas had entered. Judging by the stares turned their way, the colonel was certain that everyone was straining to hear the exchange between them.

"Not ill," the colonel said, spicing his words with a trace of indignation. "Terrified."

At this, the general cocked a bright black eye toward him; a stirring arose from the adjacent tables. "The experience has...upset her, then?"

"Why would it not?" The colonel propped his elbows on the table and clasped his hands. "A woman wakes to discover that her husband has shot and killed a man, an acquaintance, as he attempted to climb through her window. She is somewhat more than upset. She has kept to her rooms ever since that morning. She no longer feels secure in a country we both have come to think of as our home."

The general nodded, or rather tossed his head first forward, then sharply back, like a horse startled by a June bug. "Luis..." he began, hesitated, then said, "I have been told that your wife and Luis spoke often at the Palace."

"My wife speaks often to many people. Most of them have not been inspired to enter my property unannounced."

"I do not like your tone, Colonel."

"Nor do I like your implication that my wife may have been unfaithful."

Ruelas stroked his goatee, thoughtful, and then said carefully, "I am not implying it."

"I'm afraid," said the colonel, "such a neutral statement only serves to impugn my wife's honor...if not my own."

A waiter approached—Ruelas waved him angrily away. His aide sat motionless, hands in his lap, gazing at the brocaded wallpaper. Ruelas seemed flustered, as if he had not been expecting this sort of aggressiveness from the colonel.

"I have made no such imputation regarding your nephew," the colonel went on. "I am willing to subscribe to a theory that may explain his actions in a kindly light."

"And do you have such a theory?"

"Not a particular favorite. But I have heard it espoused by some that his actions were not premeditated. Perhaps it was a prank gone wrong. Or perhaps Luis was celebrating and mistook my house for that of one of his lady friends. Young men frequently commit rash acts of the sort. My point is—" Colonel Rutherford built a church and steeple with his clasped hands "—if I am willing to countenance your nephew's actions as innocent, and further to cast myself as the inadvertent villain of the piece, why are you unwilling to extend a similar courtesy to my wife?"

A vein pulsed in Ruelas' temple, but he said nothing.

"I know my wife," said the colonel with ringing sincerity. "She is a modest creature. Not worldly in the least. An honorable woman. I can bring forward innumerable witnesses who will attest to her good character. Can you produce even one who will testify that she is not as I describe?"

The silence that ensued extended throughout the restaurant. Watching Ruelas, the colonel concluded that the general had become aware of the fact that he was being forced to make a decision in public that he had planned to make in private, and he did not much like it. In effect, he had allowed the colonel to maneuver him into an ersatz trial before a jury of his peers in which the colonel served both as witness and advocate—a trial whose focus was not upon the colonel's guilt or innocence, as the general might wish it, but upon his nephew's character.

"Well, sir," the colonel said. "Will you answer?"

General Ruelas' fingers closed about the aide's salad fork, an action that the aide took notice of with a worried sidelong glance. "I cannot," said the general hoarsely.

The whispered conversations taking place in every quarter of the room swelled in volume as news of this development was passed from table to table. Elated, because it was clear that his presentation was winning the day, the colonel pressed his advantage.

"Much as I wish I might," he said, "I cannot undo the past. All I can do is to apologize for making a hasty judgment, and to regret the tragedy I have caused. And to assure you, sir, that from this day forward, your family will have in me the staunchest of allies in whatever cause they choose to support."

At this point the colonel offered his hand. It was a dicey moment. By the standards of Cuban justice, if not the letter of the law, Colonel Rutherford was in the right no matter the reason for Carrasquel's incursion upon his property. A man who did not defend the honor of his marriage was not a man. The colonel's admirable forthrightness in challenging the general's aspersions would seem to speak eloquently to the possibility that if Carrasquel and Susan had been having an affair, the colonel may not have been aware of it. If the general did not accept his hand, Colonel Rutherford had lost nothing; but he was banking on the fact that Ruelas was a realist and would ultimately decide that having a friend in high places, a friend who was in his debt, would compensate for the loss of a nephew-by-marriage who, no matter what slant one put on it, had behaved in a disgraceful fashion. Then, too, his behavior would appear less disgraceful if the general were to validate the colonel's view that Carrasquel was either drunk and misguided, or playing a prank. The colonel believed that this would prove an irresistible lure and that the general would accept the handshake, perhaps telling himself that he reserved the option to change his mind at a later date—by that time, however, the colonel suspected that he and Ruelas would be involved on many levels, on their way to becoming the best of friends.

Ruelas' eyes flitted over the silverware as if he were choosing a weapon with which to assault the colonel. But at length, albeit with a small show of bad grace, still declining to meet Colonel Rutherford's eyes, he shook the colonel's hand and said, "*Muy bien.*" He squared his shoulders, fussed with his tie, then beckoned imperiously to the waiter.

✦

Brandywines was less than half-full that night. Jimmy and Rita ate cheeseburgers at the bar, watching a Seahawks exhibition game. The Hawks were getting their asses kicked by the Jets in the first half—Coach Holmgren, walruslike in his teal and blue jacket, looked as if he'd swallowed a mouthful of bad salmon. The Seattle quarterback overthrew a screen pass, and Rita shouted, "Jesus!" and pounded the bar with the hilt of her hunting knife. "That's the guy's gonna take us to the Super Bowl? You believe this shit?"

The bartender, a glossy little man with slicked-back hair and extremely white teeth, wearing a yellow vest with black piping over a shirt with blousy sleeves, shook his head in agreement. He did not appear to know very much about football, but had become somewhat intimidated by Rita's vehemence, and now was doing his best to keep up with the game.

"Hasselbeck," she said disdainfully to Jimmy. "Y'can't have a quarterback with a name like that and expect to go to the goddamn Super Bowl!"

Jimmy had on his suede jacket and an old cowboy hat with a grease stain on the crown that he'd worn on and off ever since she had met him. The hat shadowed his face, giving him a lazy, sulky look. He stared at his fries and muttered something inaudible.

Frustrated, Rita addressed herself to the bar in general. "Lookit the guys who win Super Bowls. Kenny Stabler. Troy Aickman. Brett Favre. Joe Namath. John Elway. Solid leadership-type names. And what do we got? We got Matt fucking Hasselbeck."

"Dilfer," said a wide-shouldered fortyish man with a seamed, tired face, wearing a work shirt and a Sonics cap. Nice looking in a low-rent kind of way. He was sitting two stools farther along the bar. Rita challenged him with a stare. "What'd you say?"

"Trent Dilfer. That's a doofus name there ever was one, and he won the Super Bowl with the Ravens."

"Dilfer...Oh, yeah." Rita mulled this over, then smiled at the guy. "Fuck, I guess I'm wrong." She showed the bartender her empty glass and he hustled to bring the Jack Daniels. "Wouldn't hurt me none the son of a bitch changed his name, though."

"He can call himself Madonna for all I care, he gets us to the big game," said the man.

Rita laughed and slapped the countertop. "I wanna buy that dude a drink," she said to the bartender, who was busy pouring. "Matt Madonna. That's better than fucking Joe Montana."

Jimmy was turning out his pockets, searching for something.

Rita put a hand on his shoulder. "What's wrong, sweetie?"

He gazed at her vacantly.

"Jimmy," she said firmly. "Stop screwing around with the story and talk to me. What you looking for?"

"Loretta's address."

"It's stuck in the receipt book. I left it in the van."

A chorus of grousing came from the other patrons at the bar. Rita glanced up at the TV, now showing a replay of Hasselbeck being sacked for a huge loss. She turned again to Jimmy. "You gonna go see her?"

"Yeah...uh-huh."

Rita tossed back her whiskey. Her butt was starting to go numb, and she shifted about on the stool. "One of these days," she said morosely, watching the Seahawks' punt team running onto the field, "you gonna seriously fuck us up, y'know that?"

"I'll be back in a couple hours." His voice had acquired a soft, flat intonation, as if he were under a spell. Which, she supposed, he was. The voices of his characters squeaking at him from the tiny stage he had constructed in his head.

"I really hate this part," she said. "It's like you're in another damn dimension."

He had no response.

"You gonna space out one day and run the van into the side of a wall, you don't watch yourself."

"Okay," he said.

She dug the keys to the van out of her hip pocket, held them above her head, and with a flourish of the fingers, dropped them to clatter onto the bar. "Go on," she said. "Get outa here."

His hand swallowed the keys; he slid off his stool, straightened his jacket. "Couple hours." It seemed he was about to say something more, but he merely stood there a few seconds before heading toward the door.

Feeling apprehensive, disgruntled, Rita returned her attention to the screen. The Jets had fumbled the punt, and the Seahawks had recovered on the 23. Hasselbeck's first play from scrimmage was a pass intended for the tight end that sailed high and outside.

"This game sucks!" she said.

"It's just an exhibition game," said the man in the Sonics cap. "They'll pull it together." He toasted her with the shot she had bought him and tossed it down.

"I ain't talking bout tonight, I'm talking 'bout the NFL, man!"

Rita gobbled a handful of peanuts, chewed and talked. "Free agency ruined the game. Now you got some teams with a good offense, some with a good D, and the rest of them ain't worth a shit either way. The players switch sides every year or two. Most of the time it's like watching air hockey."

"The Ravens. Now they got Gerbach playing QB, they could be awesome."

"Fuck a bunch of Gerbach," Rita said. "What's he ever won?"

"Hey, he put up some numbers with the Chiefs."

Rita scraped up her change from the bar and stood.

"You're not leaving, are ya?" asked the man. His eyes ranged over her body. "They're gonna play that new kid at QB next quarter. Kid's supposed to be pretty good."

"Gotta make a phone call."

She threaded her way among tables to the pay phones in an alcove next to the johns. Loretta Snow's number was written on a slip of paper in her shirt pocket. She misdialed the first time, cursed, and tried again. Two rings, and then that melting-lump-of-sugar voice answered, "Hello?"

"Hey, Loretta. This is Rita Whitelaw of Guy Guns. How you doing?"

"I'm...I'm all right." Pause. "Is there a problem?"

"I'm just calling to tell ya Jimmy's comin' out to your place. He's got some business he wants to discuss."

"Oh...well...that's fine."

Oh well that's fine. Jesus. Rita had the notion she could have said Jimmy was bringing a chain saw and a body bag, and the woman would have responded in the same timid, shivery tone.

"'Member what I told you other day at the coffee cart? About you being vulnerable and all?"

Silence. Then, anxiously: "I don't want any trouble."

Rita had the urge to start banging the receiver against the wall. Get a spine, for Christ's sake!

"There ain't gonna be no trouble," she said. "The only reason I'm calling's to refresh your memory."

Another silence.

"You're a free agent, Loretta," Rita said. "You can do whatever you want. You wanna get crazy with Jimmy, that's fine by me. I'm not in the picture."

"I have no intention of getting crazy with anyone," said Ms. Snow with a tad more spine.

"Whatever you say. All I'm asking is you don't rush into things. Make an informed decision. Take a look at what you're getting into."

Rita could hear the woman breathing, pictured her dabbing at perspiration, glancing nervously about.

"This is making me very uncomfortable," Ms. Snow said.

"Well, it's almost over, honey," said Rita. "You have yourself a nice evening, now."

After breaking the connection, Rita thought of something else she might have said, but realized it wasn't worth worrying about. The man in the Sonics cap had moved himself onto the stool next to hers, and when she came up he grinned and said, "Mind if I join ya?"

"Depends what you mean by 'join,'" she said.

She sat and drained the last drop from her glass. "If you're talking about hanging out and watching the game…maybe giving me a hug whenever the Hawks score, that's fine. I get drunk enough, you might even get to second base. I'm in a funny mood and I wouldn't mind a stranger's hand on me. But you try more than that, you gonna be checking to see if you got all your fingers."

"Jesus!" The man leaned away as if to gain a clearer perspective on her. "I don't think I ever heard a woman talk like that."

"You ain't been talking to the right women." Rita looked to the TV—the Jets were preparing to punt. "Dynasties," she said. "That's what it's all about."

The man made a puzzled face.

"Back when the NFL was really fucking great, what made it great was dynasties," Rita said. "The Cowboys, the Niners. The Steelers. If you were a fan of theirs, you were high on the game all the time. If you wasn't, you hated 'em 'cause they won, and hating them made it fun." She caught sight of the man in the mirror back of the bar, hulking beside her, and gave him a playful poke in the chest. "You're part of a dynasty, y'know?"

"Me? How's that?"

"White people. You own the fucking world. You wasn't around to hate, life wouldn't make as much sense."

Jokingly, the man said, "You hate white people, how come you're messing around with me?"

"Takes all kinds, don't it?" said Rita.

✦

Lucius Shepard

Ms. Snow's residence turned out to be a pink and white house trailer parked in slot 14 of the Far West Motor Court, a dusty acreage just off the interstate surrounded by diseased-looking firs, each slot decorated with long flower boxes, many filled with bottles and cans and paper trash. Jimmy parked behind Ms. Snow's old Toyota wagon and sat with his hands on the wheel, watching her shadow moving behind the Venetian blinds. From the way she was bustling about, he had the idea she was cleaning the place. It was toil to think straight, as it always was toward the end of a story. He thought it might be a good idea to get some more of it out before talking to Ms. Snow — he didn't want to confuse things.

He drummed his fingers on the wheel, trying to find an entry, but the characters skittered out of reach, as if pissed because he hadn't been paying them notice. A light switched on in another window of the trailer, one covered by a shade, and he could see Ms. Snow in clean silhouette against it. She removed her blouse and appeared to be washing her breasts and under her arms. It was a pretty sight. Relaxing. He leaned his elbow out the window and watched. The colonel would be prone to voyeurism of this sort. Sneaking up to Susan's chambers while she was in the bath. Tiptoeing across the bedroom, holding his breath, positioning himself so he could peer in through the cracked door. At first he saw only a soapy drawn-up knee above the rim of the marble tub, but then Susan leaned forward to rinse the soap away and he was offered a view of her breasts and her face, poised and lovely in its concentration. He felt himself trembling like a hound on point and toyed with the idea of entering the bathroom and taking her. But the time was not ripe. He would have to go carefully with her, ease her back into their routine. Cautiously, he recrossed the bedroom, slipped out into the hall, gently closing the door behind. When he looked up he found Susan's maid staring at him from the head of the stair. She dropped into a curtsey and bowed her head, but he could tell she was hiding a smile. He approached and stood towering over her.

"Does something amuse you, Lupe?" he asked.
She kept her eyes lowered. "No, *Señor.*"
"I prefer you address me as Colonel."
"Your pardon, *Señ*...Colonel."
He started down the stairs, stopped, and said without turning to her. "If you're dissatisfied with your position, Lupe, I can easily make arrangements to send you back to Matanzas."
"Oh no, *Señor!* Colonel. I'm very happy!"
"I'm sure you are," he said. "But it does not make *me* happy to find you spying outside my wife's bedchamber."
"*Perdoneme, Señor.*"
"Colonel," he said. "Try not to make that mistake again."
The colonel's campaign to regain not so much his wife's affections as her dutiful obedience went slowly, but that was no more than he had anticipated. He had realized from the moment he decided to rid himself of Carrasquel that Susan would be devastated by the act, and though this was regrettable, he hoped it would allow him to rebuild her according to his design, to grind and polish her until she shined as brightly and fit as perfectly into her setting as did the ruby in his signet ring. He had known she would hate him, but he believed he would be able to wear hate down until its effectiveness was no greater than the old stubborn streak that had long kept her from absolute compliance with his wishes; and now that she was emotionally in ruins, he thought that even the stubborn streak might prove malleable to his tactics.

Gradually, over a period of weeks, he began to allow her to summon taxis and go shopping in Havana without escort. He wanted her to understand that her previous constraints had been illusory, and that it was her submissive nature that kept her from true freedom. When she would curse or otherwise abuse him, he would protest only that he had done what he had for love — could she not see it? — and then would put on a hangdog look and walk away from confrontation. But soon he took to arguing his case with more vigor, offering the logic of his actions. His late arrival at the house, his shock on encountering Carrasquel, how the recognition of what was going on, come like lightning into his mind, had shattered the prudence of his normal temper and loosed a madman. If he could travel back to that night, he told her, even knowing of the affair, he would delay his arrival so as to avoid having blood on his hands. He did not expect her to believe him, though repetition might effect a climate in which belief might grow; but he did expect that hearing the story told over and over again would abet his overall strategy of erosion.

Once the fierceness of her grief had abated, he began to bring her presents. Small ones, only. He did not wish to be perceived as offering bribes. Further, he expressed an interest in helping her gain a surer footing in life. He had not understood before, he said, how empty the days in Havana had been for her and suggested a variety of meaningful occupations: charity work, teaching in the embassy school, pastimes that would appeal to Susan's compassion and divert her from brooding. In general, he presented himself as a husband who had neglected his wife due to career concerns, but who now sought to remedy those wrongs and repair the relationship. He was aware that Susan had evidence to the contrary, but again he thought that repetition would eventually cloud the facts and make the truth of the matter difficult for her to discern.

All this, the colonel admitted to himself, was perhaps not the wisest of courses. Were he to cast his nets wide, he might well be able to secure a new wife superior to Susan in every way. She had been a constant disappointment, and even prior to the affair, he had not neglected the idea of divorce. The colonel could not quite isolate his motives in wanting to reclaim her. Certainly there was the question of appearances — an unstable marriage would have a deleterious effect on his career. Susan's undeniable physical charms were also a factor, as were the colonel's presentiment of sexual anxiety attaching to the finding of her replacement, and various other related anxieties that he chose not to examine too closely. He had no doubt that the challenge posed by Susan's collapse played into his competitive nature, but taken all in sum, these elements did not appear sufficiently compelling to sustain his endurance of a divided house and a hateful, vituperative wife.

It was at this juncture that the colonel began to wonder if he had fallen in love with Susan, if that might be the reason underlying his devotion to her rehabilitation. The notion, at first, bemused him, but the longer he pondered it, the more persuaded by it he became. He had come to enjoy nourishing his wife, and why else would he so enjoy it, but that joy was implicit to the task? These thoughts incited a flurry of mental operations—reinterpretations of events, inversions of judgments made, crucial shifts in perspective—that resulted in a total refurbishing of his view of the situation. The process was not altogether clear to him. During its initial stages he recognized that it was a tactical evasion, a trail broken onto new philosophical ground that effected a spurious enlightenment; however, by the time the process had gotten into full swing, he had lost track of this recognition and arrived at the opinion that he was in the midst of psychological reshuffling produced by the powerful emotion of the past weeks. Before too long, his original apprehension that love might be at work in him had evolved into a conviction that this was precisely the case, and, indeed, had always been the case—his courtship and marriage to Susan had been a proceeding of love, deep and abiding, only he had not realized it at the time, being too preoccupied with base desire and the prospect of obtaining a beautiful wife who would suit the requirements dictated by his career. He had been an idiot, a pompous, unfeeling ass, yet Kismet had led him nonetheless to his intended companion. Buoyed by this understanding, the colonel pressed gifts and compliments and encouragements upon his wife, and displayed ceaseless good humor in the face of her sullen acceptance. He told her he loved her at every opportunity, provoking reactions that ranged from dismay to hysteria. Love, an emotion he heretofore had foolishly not aspired to embrace, would be the salvation of them both. It soothed the incidences of guilt that infrequently came to trouble him; it increased a hundred-fold his confidence in the purity of his actions; and at last, on a night eleven weeks after the murder, it provided him the courage to visit Susan in her bedchamber.

Armed, then, with love, and also with the knowledge that his campaign had drained much of the venom from Susan's store, he entered the chamber at half past nine, dressed, as it happened, exactly as he had been on the morning of the murder—in braces, undershirt, and trousers. In his hand he carried the Colt, holstered to show he intended her no harm. A warm orange radiance issued from a bedside lamp with a shade fashioned of pumpkin-colored glass, shaped into leaf-shaped sections by lead mullions, and on the bed, a canopied white float enclosed in mosquito netting, Susan lay atop the covers, wearing a green silk robe and reading. When she saw the colonel, her features went slack and she said, "No," in a weak voice and turned back to her book.

Ignoring the rejection, the colonel pushed aside the netting and sat on the edge of the bed. Gently, so as not to disturb her. "I want you," he said in a voice welling with emotion.

Susan squeezed her eyes shut. "Please…"

Keeping his voice pitched soft, he said, "I can't live this way, Susan. I love you, I need to touch you."

She held the book so as to shield her breasts and shook her head slowly back and forth.

"We have to move forward," he said. "I understand that I've been neglectful. I was…"

"Neglectful?" She laughed brokenly. "You think you have been neglectful?"

"Yes," he said. "Neglect is at the matter's heart. And neglect had been father to…" He struggled with the word; she seemed so precious to him now, it wounded him to be reminded of their past. "Cruelty," he went on. "I admit that

I've been cruel. What was in my mind, I cannot recall. It strikes me now that I was afraid of you."

Disbelief in her face, she stared at him, lips parted, her blue eyes full of light. It was as if, he thought, she failed to recognize him, or—and this he hoped to be the case—she were seeing him anew.

"I have always been somewhat unbending," he said, lowering his head. "I was afraid of becoming...close. I thought you would not respect me if I were not Colonel Rutherford—" he made the name into an epithet. "And I feared also were I to divest myself of that pose, I might never inhabit it again and thus would lose the respect of everyone." He made a fist and placed it against his temple. "It galls me to think of it. How I could have valued such an empty treasure as respect. It means nothing to me now. All I want is your forgiveness, your love."

At the word "love," Susan's dumbfounded expression collapsed into a stony mask. "I hate you!" she said in a witch's whisper. "How can you come to me like this? God!"

The colonel's chest constricted, his eyes misted. He composed himself and said, "Very well. If you hate me...here." He drew the Colt from its holster and laid it beside her hip. "Take it. Finish me. I will not live this way."

She stared avidly at the gun for a long moment; she glanced up at the colonel, then back to the gun.

"Take it," he said.

Susan's face appeared to crumble, then to become suffused with horror, and the colonel realized that she must have recognized the Colt to be the weapon with which he had shot Carrasquel.

"Here." He picked up the Colt and held the barrel to his chest. "All you need do is touch the trigger. The pressure required is very slight."

The fingers of her right hand, still pressed to the cover of her book, flexed, and he thought that she might accept his sacrifice; but she offered no gesture toward the gun and turned her head sharply away, so he could not read her expression.

He set the Colt on the table, shifted nearer and leaned across her, bracing his right hand on the bed beside her waist—in effect, pinning her there. "We must go forward with our lives, Susan," he said. "We cannot continue as we are."

Cautiously, he bent and kissed the angle of her neck. She stiffened. With gentle hands, he pried the book from her grasp, and it, too, he set aside. He kissed the point of her jaw, eliciting from his wife an indrawn breath, and undid the belt of her silk robe. She did not respond to his kisses, his touches, other than to comply with his more urgent movements—but he had not hoped for more. To do so would be premature. With tenderness and loving concern, he encouraged her to join with him, and when at last he lay between her legs and her flesh gave way, the colonel felt an immeasurable, an altogether unprecedented, degree of satisfaction.

✦

Except for a plastic baseball bat poking out from beneath the sofa, the living room of Ms. Snow's trailer exhibited no sign of recent habitation. It was filled with yard-sale furniture, and the stained plywood paneling was decorated with wall hangings of the sort you might find in K-Mart: a tiger prowling a lurid red night through a black and gold jungle; an electric-looking Christ dying for the world's sins; and, unexpectedly, John Lennon posed as an angel. The place was spotless, neat, plaid throw pillows arranged on a turquoise-colored sofa and magazines spread on the coffee table, just as you might find in a catalogue photo. Ms. Snow wore a pink housedress with little cherry blossoms all over, showing a hint of cleavage. She smelled of flowery water. She led Jimmy to the sofa, had him sit, and then perched at the opposite end, pushed up against the arm. "If I'd known you were coming," she said, "I'd have gone to the store. All I have to offer you is juice and—" she smiled apologetically "—Kool-Aid."

"I'm okay," Jimmy said, removing his hat.

"Let me take that."

Before he could object, she snatched the hat from him and walked across the room to set it on the counter that divided living room from kitchen. He liked the way she moved. Quick but fluid. The pink dress flouncing with the roll of her hips. She sat back down and her smile flickered on. "Do you have some news for me?"

The feathery dark hairs she had trained down beside her ears to create the effect of sideburns held his attention, and he let a few seconds go by before he answered. "Yeah," he said. "Kinda."

Her posture smartened, and she looked at him with eagerness, knees together, hands clasped, waiting.

"The professor faxed me a bid," he said. "Seven thousand. And Borchard come back with seven-five."

"Seven thousand would be..." Ms. Snow cast her eyes to the ceiling, to heaven, and sighed. "Wonderful."

"That ain't seven thousand for you, y'know. With my twenty percent, that gets you fifty-six hundred."

"It's still more than I hoped to get," she said firmly.

"We can probably squeeze a little more. I figure the professor might go to eight, I talk it up right. Give you another eight hundred dollars."

She put a hand to her cleavage, as if to quell the beating of her heart, and he tracked the gesture. "I want to thank you, Mister..." She tipped her head, gave him an appealing look. "Is it okay if I call you Jimmy. Mister Guy is so..."

"Sounds like a name they'd give a protein drink or something," he said. "Yeah, Jimmy's good."

"And I'm Loretta."

She stuck out her hand for a shake. It was like holding a piece of warm, delicately carved soapstone, soft and strong.

"You've been a salvation, Jimmy. We're going to keep you in our prayers from now on."

Lucius Shepard

The "we" perplexed him—then he recalled the plastic bat.

"Kids are asleep, huh?"

"Yes! Thank God!" She hopped up off the couch and went for the kitchen. "I just remembered! I've got vodka. It's been in the freezer so long, I'd forgotten all about it." She opened the freezer. "Would you join me in a little celebration?"

"I don't know it's such a good idea to celebrate before you got something to put in the bank."

"Well, I do." She returned with the vodka bottle and two glasses, which she placed on the coffee table. She gave him the plain one and kept one with a partly rubbed-off Pokemon figure on the side for herself. "I haven't had anything to celebrate for so long…" She poured a stiff measure into his glass, leaning toward him as she did, the pink cloth falling away from her chest, revealing the slope of a plump breast encased in satiny cloth and lace. She poured herself about a finger and lifted the glass to him. "Thank you," she said in a quiet voice. "Thank you so much."

"Just business," he said.

They sipped, then set their glasses down on the table in almost perfect unison.

"You must do a lot of traveling," she said after a silence.

"Well, we do and we don't," he said, leaning back. "We hit the shows in Yakima, Missoula, Boise, Sand Point. Pretty much all over the Northwest. Don't seem much like traveling to me. But once or twice a year we do a national show. In LA or Las Vegas. One time in New York."

"I'll bet that was exciting."

"It ain't like we got time to see the sights. Mostly it's we fly in, do the show, and fly out again. Course Rita likes to hit the bars. She loves finding a new bar to tear up."

"I imagine you meet a lot of interesting people," Ms. Snow said with less vivacity.

"Some," said Jimmy, and tried to think of them—the only one he could come up with at first was a guy he'd run into in Billings who could stand next to a school bus and shoot his

100

piss clear over the roof of the thing. Then his brain served up a better candidate. "There was a fella in LA. A producer. He was after me to do technical advising on some movie, and he invited us to a party. He had this big ol' house in the hills with a deck and a pool. About five minutes after we got there, we met up with Kevin Costner."

"You did?" Ms. Snow gave "did" two syllables. "I love him! What was he like?"

"Didn't seem like all that much to me. He grabbed my hand and tried to bust it off, then he gave me a real sincere smile...Y'know, kinda smile a preacher gives ya when he's sizing up your wallet. He was took with Rita, though. He dragged her off into a corner and tried to impress her with his knowledge of Indian lore. I thought she was gonna rip him a new one, but she played along. She acted all impressed, like 'Ooh, Mister Costner, you're so smart! My people're so grateful for all your service to them.' Then she got to telling him about Blackfoot ways. Just filling his head with absolute horseshit. Costner was so into her, he started taking notes. It was funnier than hell."

Ms. Snow laughed politely. "Did you meet any other movie stars?"

"There was a guy used to be somebody on TV, but I can't recall the show. He was all the time making funny faces."

Ms. Snow said, "Maybe it was Jim Carrey," and Jimmy told her that the guy had been chubby and about sixty. Having exhausted his immediate supply of interesting people, he prodded Ms. Snow to tell about herself. She said there wasn't much to tell, but as was the case with most people in the habit of saying that, she proceeded to tell it all. It was like he'd tapped a keg and didn't have a stopper. She told him about her kids—Brandy, Job, and Celine (for her favorite singer), ages eight to twelve—and her job as an apprentice beautician (in Seattle she'd be full-fledged and licensed), and about her church (The Church of Apostolic Union over in Kent), and about the pet cat who'd recently had a fatal encounter with a yuppie in a Beamer. The passion with which she invested these meager details fascinated Jimmy. She was a woman, he realized, whose passion had been kept down for quite a while. Every gesture and expression embodied a release of furious energy. Her voice, though it remained shaky and frail, seemed to tremble as a result of strength, as if the instrument were too weak to carry the freight of emotion. In her enthusiasm, she shifted closer to him. Her top button had come undone, and when she leaned forward he could see the shape of a nipple pushing against the fabric of her bra. The sight muddled him, knocked down a wall in his mental storehouse, and things kept separate tumbled together. One of the characters in his story stepped forward and slipped him a thought. It had been so long...so very, very long. He shook himself to restore focus. Ms. Snow never noticed. She was off onto a trip she and the kids had taken to Vancouver Island, saying how someone had tried to sell marijuana to her oldest. The whole island was nothing but dope growers and sex maniacs. Someone had told her they had nude drug festivals twice a year. Eventually the engine of her conversation sputtered and died, gasping out a final few exaggerations about crime in Canada, and they sat without speaking. Jimmy's character kept sticking his nose in, offering suggestions, observations. How forlorn she seemed, so unlike the girl he had played with late into the summer dusk, a smell of boxwood thickening the air...

Jimmy slammed the door on his story, glanced at Ms. Snow. She stole a peek at him, let out a disappointed-sounding sigh, as if to say, "Oh, well. Guess that's that." The only way he could think to keep the evening going was more business.

"There's something else we should go over," he said.

She straightened, freshly alert.

"I got a feeling we could jump Borchard up into five figures and get you a serious stake. He's dying for that Colt."

"No," she said, laying the word out there like a stone on top of a casket.

His character demanded the floor—Jimmy shouldered the door shut again. "I know your objections," he said. "But it might be the best way to get him gone. He'd be satisfied, and you'd wind up with maybe near twice as much money."

She tucked a strand of hair into place behind her ear and sat primly, tightly gathered. "You don't understand."

"Try me," he said.

"He calls me three, four times a day..." She broke off, fighting back tears.

How beautiful and strong she was in her sadness. Emotion might grip her, but she would always shrug it off and go on. The character's thought was so similar to his own, Jimmy didn't bother kicking him to the curb.

"He calls you?" He touched her arm, consoling. "Why didn't you say so?"

"You don't understand! You can't tell him anything—he does whatever he wants." Her voice deteriorated into a sob. "Every time he calls he talks about how he's gonna hurt me and the kids if he doesn't..." The tears came, their weight bearing down her head.

"Thought you was gonna get in touch if he bothered you?"

She was weeping profusely now, unable to speak. He eased closer, draped an arm about her shoulder, and she collapsed against him.

"All right. Settle down," he said. "We ain't selling to him."

She lifted her face to him, and there it was, the yearning, expectant look he'd been hoping for...years of hope, years of silent endurance and despondency. Her cobalt eyes went down for miles. He kissed her, and she turned into the kiss, looped her arms about his neck. His left hand fitted to her waist, thumb pressuring the side of her breast, rubbing the undercurve. He kissed the hollow of her throat, fingered a button and popped it free. She gave a melodious cry, the last gentle note of a despairing music, and deepened the kiss. His fingers worked feverishly, advantaging himself of her abandoned resolve. Between the lace-trimmed cups of her

Lucius Shepard

undergarment was a snap, and when he disengaged it, her breasts spilled forth, a plush, almost indescribable softness nuzzling his palms. "Oh, cousin," he whispered, his mind drugged with warmth and beauty. His hand fell to her knee, slid higher until he touched the core of her warmth, the convulsed secret she had finally dared to reveal. He wanted the scent of her, the taste, and lowered her to lie upon the couch. "My beautiful cousin," he said, pushing the dress up past her hips. The lacy white mound of her sex. The inside of one thigh glistening and damp.

"Wait!" She pushed at him with the heel of her hand. A weak push, but it muddied his waters, and though she kept on speaking, he couldn't hear her at first.

"...cousin?" she said, and waited; then: "Well, why?" He didn't catch her meaning.

"Why'd you call me 'cousin?'" she said insistently.

He felt like a man whose baggy clothes were flapping in a high wind and was trying to hold himself together. "Just a habit. Y'know, like a family thing."

Tension ebbed from her face, but not altogether.

"Guess I'm feeling close to you," he said..

"I know." A smile melted up. "Me, too." She kissed him pertly, clasped her hands behind his neck, inviting him closer.

He chose a mole on her white shoulder for his mark, pressed his lips there, then to the upper slope of a breast. She quickened, her breath shallow. He flicked his tongue across the nipple and whispered, "I love you." Her body stiffened against him. "All these years," he said. "I never thought this night would come." Her sugary voice answered, but there was a singing in his ears, the rush of blood and heat, and he couldn't hear. He imagined she was saying the same word his blood sang, love over and over. "There is no wrong in this, cousin," he said. "We are of one blood *and* one heart." Then she was pulling at his hair, slapping, hurting him.

"What're you talking about?" she cried, shoving him away. She struggled up, bunched handfuls of the pink dress to hide her glorious breasts. She gazed at him with confu-

104

sion and dread. "I want you to leave," she said. "I'm sorry, but I…I just want you to leave."

He sat mutely, watching shattered pieces of the moment fly outward beyond the corners of his eyes. The head of his erection was jammed against his jeans—he resisted the urge to adjust it.

"Will you please go?" She had begun to weep again, and he wanted to comfort her, but the old restraints were back, iron bands clamped about his arms, his tongue.

"Oh, God! You're not going to be like him, are you?" She let the dress slide from her breasts and tucked in her elbows to cover them, buried her face in hands.

He wondered briefly who "him" might be, then said, "I was merely responding to your summons."

She peered at him over the tips of her fingers, terrified. She shut her eyes. "Please…please please please go!" The words were squeezed out, as if they were the dregs of her resistance.

He got clumsily to his feet, swayed, searched for his hat. His tread shook glassware in a kitchen cabinet. He scooped the hat up from the counter, held it in both hands. "Forgive me," he said.

She refused to look at him.

"All right," he said. "All right."

The cold air shocked him—he had dressed for a warmer climate. He walked unsteadily away from the place, unable to think of a destination, a heaviness in his chest. He recognized nothing of the night.

"Mister Guy!"

The name alerted Jimmy. He turned to the trailer. The door was cracked to show a line of light thin as a crosshair. He wasn't entirely clear about what was going on.

Ms. Snow said, "Would you mind next time when there's business letting Rita handle it?"

★

He drove the van recklessly, speeding through slow zones, stomping on the brakes at lights. He was less upset over what had happened than anxious for it not to happen again until he reached the motel. Five, maybe six miles from the trailer court, he began to think character thoughts, to see the imagined. Worried that he might lose control of the van, he pulled into the lot of a closed-for-business drive-in with a tall sign on the roof from which the neon lettering had been removed. The windows blank and lightless, booths vacant, counters dusty and littered with old packaging. He killed the engine, sat staring into the abandoned place, peopling it with sore-ankled waitresses; amphetamine-edged truck drivers; three kids working on the downside of a blotter trip, laughing at the menu and the blotchy colors on each other's faces; seniors looking for a conversation with a stranger, something to remember of an unmemorable day. This time he didn't have to search for a way into the story. It bore down on him like an angry old man waving a stick, chasing ordinary thoughts off, as if they were barn cats sprinting for cover, and then he was with Susan, wandering the swamps of grief. Looking for something that would reconnect her to life, and finding it in the cold airless regions of hate where, distant from everything, her judgments refined, made icy, she could withstand the howling emptiness that poured up from the grave.

Hate perfected itself in Susan's heart more efficiently than had love. Whereas lóve had possessed her, hate was something she possessed, something she could wield. She imagined it at first to have the likeness of a gleaming steel needle revolving on end and growing sharper with every turn, hovering inside her, lit by a mysterious radiance like a relic on museum display. But as grief faded...No, faded was not the right word, not the word she would use. As grief merged with her, the way a shroud over time will rot and combine with the rotting flesh it surrounds, becoming one substance, she learned to view hate as an organic quality that sprouted from a rich soil fertilized by grief. Whatever its nature, it was more easily satisfied than love, and perhaps more durable, though of this last she was not certain. Her love for Luis seemed undimmed, as if it took its charge from an entirely different source. It was smaller now, not—as it had been—a vast cloud in which she wandered, but rather a cloud adrift inside her. Yet she had no doubt that if she were, through some art of God's, to encounter him on the street or at the Palace, everything she felt would suddenly be enlarged and she would be lost again.

Each morning she would sit at her writing desk, poring over his letters and poems, lingering over those passages in which he most lived, so that she, too, could live. But time and again she encountered passages that disturbed her nostalgia, sentences fraught with anxiety and pain, and with intimations of a tragedy to come:

I have followed you
along a trail of obsession
to the edge of my life
where a solitary star broods
above a blood-dark sea
spilling into a void
into which furniture
galleons and diamonds
centuries and horses
are also falling endlessly
and there you hover
beyond the last firm ground
daring me to leap…

This particular passage, from one of his final poems, reminded her how greatly her indecisiveness had contributed to his death, and that was sufficient to shift her attention away from love and inspire her to contemplate the products of hate.

The colonel had cut back on his traveling, and thus claimed his husbandly rights with increasing frequency. She would lie in bed, in the dark, pretending to sleep, dreading the peremptory sound of his knock, and when he entered, conceding that she had lost the right to deny him by virtue of her failure to take the Colt from his hand; she would feign a sleepy acceptance, her thoughts clenched like a fist, trying not to notice his heaviness, the antiseptically perfumed flavor of his mouth, his fumbling caresses, his grunting mastery, how even in his lust he conveyed a mechanical style. But notice these things she did. She could no longer, as once she had, pretend that the colonel was Luis—it was too monstrous a pretense now. Her only refuge lay in denial. After he left she would wash his stink from her skin and sit staring blindly out into the shadowy confusion of the grounds, hopeless and uncaring. At times she felt an unraveling within her, a loss of cohesion, and worse, she also felt the urge to surrender to this dissolution. Madness could be no more cruel than her current existence, which seemed a colorless nightmare by day, and by night a vivid one. Her life, she believed, was over.

Four months after the murder she received a letter from her cousin Aaron. She did not bother to open it immediately. They corresponded regularly now, but she was past needing a confidante. At any rate, Aaron had proved a disappointment in the role. He lectured too much, his advice was always the same—"Leave!"—and lately a distinct note of ardor been creeping into his writing. She had yet to tell him of the circumstances surrounding Luis' death, because she knew his response would have little value.

Eventually, for want of any more compelling pastime, she opened Aaron's letter. The first few paragraphs were as expected—news of his business, projections of growth, plans for expansion. But on the second page, the tone of the letter changed:

> ...I can no longer refrain from speaking what is in
> my heart. When we began this correspondence, I
> informed you that I was not certain whether some
> portion of the feelings I once expressed to you still

remained. I believed, however, that if they did, it would be in the form of a dark residue, a shadow of what was. But your letters, dear Susan, and the memories they conjure have proved the lie of this. What I perceived to be a shadow was a merely an accumulation of dark time and darker shame, a covering I contrived to hide an emotion that even I, to whom it seems natural and true, know is wrong, and it is as strong in me now as ever it was. I fully expect that you will wish to end our correspondence after hearing this news, and I will not seek to influence you to the contrary. Perhaps that is for the best. I cannot think that this renewal of an emotion I assumed to be moribund, if not dead, can have any benefit for either of us...

Susan let the letter fall listlessly from her hand. She had grown weary of Aaron's self-absorption and she did not have the patience to read through what looked to be several more pages of confession and analysis. Only Aaron, she thought, could make an incestuous passion seem boring. Even when they were young and lively in their play, he had always exhibited a mature sense of incaution, carefully balancing the joys of every mischief against the potentials of the woodshed, as if already studying for his career in accounting. Thus it had amazed her all the more when he had initially announced his love—how had a man so frightened of her father's hand dared such iniquity? He must, she told herself, have truly loved her. And, by his own declaration, he still did. If she had known that evening in the garden what she knew now, offered a choice between contemptible perversion and a future with Colonel Rutherford, she believed she would have opted for the former...This sentiment, though it came as whimsy, lingered in her thoughts, as if begging for her notice, and when, upon examining it more closely, she realized its implications, she was inclined to reject out of hand the scenario it engendered—yet it was so perfect a design, so potent a deceit, she could not completely dismiss it. She sought to peer inside herself, trying to find the spiritual lesion that she knew must exist or else she would never have come to reflect upon this evil machination. She seemed in all particulars herself, every portion of her psyche in, if not good, then at least working, order. Yet she was unable to accept this self-judgment. Something must have changed, some vial of glandular poison spilled, subtly affecting the heart of her nature; otherwise she could never have entertained that serpent of an idea slithering joyfully about her brain, infecting every cell with its flicking kiss.

She deliberated for more than an hour before deciding that the idea was a gift from the Serpent Himself, the Prince of Betrayals. Not that God was incapable of such a gift. Had He not given her over to the ministrations of an unctuous, murderous devil...and for no meet purpose? But this idea had scales, fangs, and a flexible spine that permitted it to coil up in her heart and nest—it was the Devil's tongue inside her, moving her to act, and though she feared for her soul, she had lost the necessary resolve to resist the Serpent's incessant stimulation. She plucked her silver pen from its holder and began to write, telling Aaron how Luis had died, embellishing the tale with every possible flourish, and when she had done with that, she inscribed the following line:

> ...As to the greater substance of your letter, dear cousin, and I speak here of your newly confessed emotion, it both shames and delights me to tell you that I, too, have a confession to make, one long overdue, of feelings kept in secret, unexpressed, yet still vital to my heart's progress...

She filled three pages with her lie, confabulating a history of yearning and frustration, feeling shame in the act, yet exulting in its commission. When she finished, she felt oddly aloof and uncaring, as if by taking this step she had taken herself beyond the reach of conscience. She knew that, ultimately, guilt would find her again, but she had sealed a bargain with a power compared to which guilt was a mere shadow.

> ...In October, as is his habit each year, Hawes will travel with a manservant to the mountains of Matanzas where he keeps a lodge, and there, in a frenzy of bloodletting, will gun down every wild pig in the vicinity, an act that to my mind seems verging on self-slaughter. He will be gone ten days, longer if the sport is good. Would it be importune of me to ask that you visit Havana during this time, so I might then sway whatever doubts you harbor of me by the most persuasive of my means...?"

✦

On Monday, Rita manned the tables most of the day. Jimmy was in a state, sitting in a folding chair with his back turned to the show, legs stretched out, unmoving and unspeaking, as if rigor had set in. He stirred himself once to deal with a gun question from a customer, and at noon he ambled off to fetch her a sandwich and returned an hour and a half later with a corn dog and vague answers as to where he had been. She was used to him being worthless from time to time, and she wasn't that concerned. Between the Colt and the Beretta and, fingers crossed, the Thompson, by tonight they would be in better shape than they'd been in for a long while. And then there was Yakima coming up— they always did well in Yakima, and she loved going to McGallagher's and getting the dick of every white boy in the place twirling like a propeller on a toy plane, luring them away from their pale, flabby female counterparts.

The crowd was thin but all business. The long-haired kids dreaming of death were off partying, as were the souvenir hunters and the NRA moms and pops. Dealers were shaving their profit margins, big checks were changing hands, smiles everywhere. Around three-thirty, a guy from the armory offices brought her a fax from Professor Alex Howle, offering eleven thousand for the Colt and the shakily authenticated but intriguing pistol he had displayed interest in when he had seen them in Spokane—he could wire cash if they wished. Rita had no clue which pistol he meant. She crumpled up an empty styrofoam cup and tossed it at Jimmy's head. Not a twitch. "Jimmy!" she said, turning the name into a flinty grunt. "Fucking wake up!" He drew in his legs, scrunched about in the chair, said, "Huh?"

"I need you. Clear your fucking head!"

He scraped his chair around a quarter-turn, managing it sluggishly. Then another quarter-turn, so he was facing the aisle. She passed him the fax. He studied the paper for longer than necessary.

"Any day now," Rita said.

"Yeah," he said, nodding. "I mean, I was wanting more for the pistol—here he's getting it for 'bout two-thirds what I figured on. But it's cash money, and we won't have to pay taxes on none of it."

"What pistol's he talking 'bout?"

"Nineteen-thirty-two Smith and Wesson. The Klan gun."

"It don't have to be we getting eight-five for the Colt. We could shave that down a little. Loretta would still come out fine."

"Naw," he said, staring her down. "That wouldn't be fine."

Fuck you, she thought. You and your little white-ass chicken.

"I'm gonna go fax the professor," she said. "Then I'm gonna take a shower, get me some food, and party. You can handle the last hour."

His face showed he was readying a complaint.

"You got time to work on the damn story after closing," she said. "Don't pack nothing. I'll take care of it in the morning." She stood and wedged herself out between tables. "You better call Borchard. Tell him whatever you gonna."

"Already talked to him."

"Yeah, but you didn't have this fax when you did."

"Don't matter. He said he wanted me to come see him after his meeting one way or another." He hesitated. "Guess I can just call him, though."

"You go on up and see the man. He might have something interesting to say."

Jimmy fiddled with the corner of a leaflet someone had left on the table. "Where you gonna be?"

From the faded quality of his voice, she realized he was about to go drifting again. They'd be lucky if somebody didn't steal them blind. But she was suddenly fed up with faxes and money and guns and dipshits in need of home protection.

"You gonna hafta find me tonight," she said, "'cause I plan to get myself lost."

He looked so forlorn, she relented a bit.

"I ain't guaranteeing nothing," she said. "But I'll be starting out at Gainer's."

✦

A band name of Mister Right was laying waste to Gainer's, a roadhouse ten minutes from Issaquah, shaking dust down from the ceiling of that chunk of pale blue cement block with neon Red Hook displays in the windows and everything from pickups to SUVs to a brand-new Mercedes in the jammed-up lot. By the time Rita arrived, just past ten, a drizzle was pocking the dusty lanes between the parked cars, and half-a-dozen fools too drunk to get in were pushing and shoving and falling down laughing out front of the door. They sobered some when they saw Rita step out of her cab. She knew she looked good, wearing her black mesh see-thru blouse over a black bra, and she acted like she knew it, rolling her hips to the monstrous 4/4 leaking from the inside. She didn't know yet what part she would play, but nonetheless she was starting to get a feeling for the role. One of the fools, a hairless baby bear with a shaved head and a purple Huskies jersey, grabbed at her ass, but she danced out of reach and tossed him a mocking look as she passed into the noise and darkness.

She worked her way through the crowd at the bar, pushed up against the rail of the waitress station by shifting bodies. She could just make out the heads of the band above the crowd on the dance floor, hot white stage lights behind them. The dancing was for shit. People lumbering, lurching about like cave folk round a gutted elk. Boys in Dockers and polo shirts shaking their fists; girls in short tight dresses making fishlike motions with their hips. Her eyes began to adjust to the dimness. Glowing wreaths of cigarette smoke floated in air. There were tables at the center and back of the place; sticking out from the walls were little counters, each one ranged by four or five stools. Men groping compliant women. Women leaning their heads together and laughing hysterically, saying shit like, "Do you believe it?" and calling each other "girlfriend." Womanless men sharking among the tables or trying to look blasé as they sat nursing a beer. She remembered a line from an old story of Jimmy's: "...a zooful of brown passions." That's what Gainers was tonight. Nothing much could happen there. A fistfight, a break-up, some meaningless hook-ups, a carload of drunks crashing on the way home. Rita figured to tune the intensity a notch higher.

Mister Right crunched into a heavy groove rendition of an old Massive Attack song, and Rita danced along with it, holding onto the rail, lowering her head and letting her hair curtain her face, doing a step that was ninety percent ass-shaking and the rest sliding her feet as if she were tired and hanging onto a slow-moving treadmill. A bedraggled-looking waitress elbowed her way up to the station, scribbled an order on her tray. "Hey!" Rita shouted. The waitress offered her an ear and Rita passed her a twenty and shouted again, "Double shot Cuervo Gold and a draft!" When the drinks came she threw down half the tequila and had a swallow of beer. A guy at the bar was scoping her, but she didn't want him. She sipped her beer, eyes roaming the room. Close to the edge of the dance floor, one of the counters was empty; the stools that had ringed it appropriated by the seven people gathered about the adjoining counter. Four women, three men. Twenty-somethings. Promising, she thought. She weaved her way through the tables, holding the drinks above her shoulders to avoid spillage, and when she reached the empty counter, she made it her home and leaned against the wall. Three of the twenty-something women were sitting with their backs to her. Two brunettes sandwiching a blond with a double-wide butt. The brunette farthest away sneaked a glance at Rita. She was coarsely pretty, shiny hair pulled back from her face, a blood-red, too-full mouth, and makeup caking the acne blemishes on her cheeks. She had on a skin-tight hoochie dress, and as she talked she used her body freely, throwing up her arms, shimmying her breasts and her shoulders, putting on a show. But there was a hint of tight-ass in the eyes. Rita tagged her as a blow-job queen. BJ.

She fended off a lone wolf, stood moving with the music, and then started eye-fucking the guy at the end of the adjoining counter. A lanky sandy-haired guy with the open, handsome face of young Corporate America. His long muscles weren't a product of gym work. Must have played some ball. Worn jeans and a black T-shirt without advertisement. He looked to Rita like he came from money — money dressed plain when it was out slumming. He smiled at her, revealing perfect capped teeth, and his eyes seemed to empty out. My brother, Rita thought. She looked away, as if offended. Then she smiled, too. BJ caught his arm, drew him into a shouted conversation, but he kept on checking out Rita, and after the band took a break, the jukebox kicking in at a lower volume, he called out, "Wanta join us?"

Rita shrugged, mouthed Okay, sidled over. The sandy-haired guy surrendered his stool to her. "Walter!" he said, tapping his chest.

"Lisa!" She said it so they all could hear. The fourth woman was another brunette, small and doll-like, who was holding the hand of an equally small curly-haired man. They had their own world going, exchanging secrets, in diminutive union against the tall. The third guy was heavier and shorter than Walter, his hair lighter, Germanic stock, wearing gray slacks, a red golf shirt without a crest or an alligator or any such bullshit on the pocket. His watch was platinum, ultrathin. Rita concluded that he and Walter were out trolling together, they'd run into the doll couple, and maybe the doll woman knew BJ and the blond, whose name turned out to be Janine. She looked like money, too. A collegiate-type plaid blouse and skirt, but a very expensive gold bracelet. She would have been a hottie if she dropped thirty pounds and slacked off on the cocaine. The skin above her sinuses was islanded with inflamed blotches. Seated next to her against the wall: Dee, short for Denise. Very pale; hair down her back; probably the youngest. Dressed in jeans and a UCAL Golden Bears T-shirt that fit like a nightgown. Rita's first impression was that she was a mouse, but she came to realize that Dee was white-girl exotic. Enormous dark eyes, a dainty nose, a mouth that was sculpture. A face as carefully bred as an Afghan's, all clever angles and artful hollows. She wore no makeup and rarely spoke.

Their conversation eddied around Rita. It consisted of gossip and boasts and sexual innuendo, fleshed out with a litany of catch phrases. BJ asked Rita what she did, and Rita said, "I'm an actress." Except for Dee, who displayed pointed interest, their reaction was a studied neutrality. "I do Native American parts," Rita added. Smiles and nods. Now they understood.

"You filming around here?" Walter asked.

She shook her head. "I'm not working. Just running around visiting friends in the area." She grinned. "I'm on a whirlwind tour. But I'm doing a picture in Canada with Liam Neeson next month."

"Yeah? What's it called?" This from Walter's Teutonic friend.

"They gone through a half-dozen titles. When I got the script, it just said 'Bigfoot Script' on the cover."

"It's about Bigfoot?" Janine was amused. Dee gazed at Rita with transparent envy.

"It ain't as dumb as it sounds." Rita rebuked herself for the "ain't," but nobody seemed to notice. "It's an eco-thriller. Liam plays a scientist. Everybody thinks he's a nut. He believes Bigfoot exists, spends all his time in the wilderness hunting for sign. Eventually he finds them and starts livin' with them. Like that woman over in Africa."

"Goodall," Janine said authoritatively.

"Whatever. Anyway, Liam tries to prevent 'em from bein' captured. It's got a huge budget. You should see the makeup for the bigfeet. Incredible! And they signed Charlize Theron as the love interest."

"You're not the love interest?" Walter asked.

"Sweet thing!" She patted his cheek. "No, I play a wise Indian woman who knows the secrets of the forest. I sacrifice myself to help Liam in the third act." She winked at them. "But I come back as a ghost in the end."

She snagged a passing waitress, handed her a credit card. "Run a tab on this, will ya?" She glanced at others. "Tequila okay?"

Tequila it was.

They were all impressed. Usually they were the dispensers of largesse. They respected its uses.

It was easy after that. The band came back onstage and Rita enticed her new best friends into a drinking game. The doll people begged off, said they had to drive. But the others played along. Walter never lost, but drank a couple of shots to be polite. He smiled frequently—the expression transformed his face into a mask hiding a sickly glare. Dee lost once. After draining her glass, she looked at Rita and screwed up her face and grinned. All her looks had begun going Rita's way. Walter's friend, Janine, and BJ lost with regularity, but it was Janine who showed the effects. She became sloppy affectionate, hugging BJ and Dee...Dee more often. The two women had a distinct dynamic. Whenever Dee spoke, Janine looked fondly, dotingly at her, as if proud of a child for reciting her lines, and Dee would refuse to acknowledge her look. Until, that is, Janine got sick. Everyone ministered to her then, and finally BJ hustled her outside for some air.

The band launched a mid-tempo rocker — Walter asked Rita if she cared to dance. She hauled him down by the neck, shouted in his ear: "I'm saving you for later!" He pulled back and smiled his serial-killer smile. Rita downed a shot, slipped off the stool. She invited Dee to dance by beckoning with both hands, swaying her hips. Dee was startled, pleased, but she waved to signal, No. Rita frowned and mouthed C'mon, beckoning again. Okay. Dee hopped off her stool, proving to be taller than Rita. She took Rita's hand. The doll people were shocked.

They found room to dance near the stage, directly beneath Mister Right's bassist, a sleepy-eyed Chicano guy with a soul patch. The music gloved Rita, squeezed her like a kitten in its fist. All the pressure built up over the past days flowed out of her, convulsing her hips, shaking her breasts. Dee danced the same as most of the white girls, her hands holding the thick waist of an invisible partner, hips working off the down beat. Rita wanted to loosen her up. She danced closer and rested her hands on Dee's hips. The girl's eyes widened, but she went with it. Rita guided her, eventually got her moving less like a hinged stick. Nearby couples stared then looked away. Lesbians were cool. Weird, but cool. Political correctness a jingle in their heads. The band segued into a salsa rhythm, probably a sop to the bass player. A conga drummer had joined them, coming out from the wings — he was a bitch, a genuine music monster, pulling beats from the skin with his bandaged fingers, speedy gunfire riffs. Rita showed Dee what to do, and this was the music the girl had needed. Her body responded with shoulders, butt, hips twisting, making that baggy shirt move as if a live crazy woman was inside it. Her hair fanned out behind her like a black peacock's tail. Rita kept a hand on her, held her tight so their breasts nudged, then not quite releasing her, fingertips touching, letting her solo. Then more tightly, linking her hands behind the girl's ass, doing a grind against her thigh. Their faces inches apart. Dee was locked in on her, flushed, and Rita felt her yielding, resistance an energy discharging from her waist. The music was a bubble around them, trapping them at its silent heart. Rita airbrushed a kiss onto that wide, dreamy mouth, just a pass of the lips, a spray of sensation. Dee's lips parted, and Rita took the cue, tongue-fucked her a little, a quick taste. She drew back and they did it with their eyes, Dee going all cherry soulful and sweet. When the music ended, she jumped up and down and applauded. "Want some coke?" she shouted to Rita. "Come on!" She skipped backwards in front of Rita on the way to the ladies' john, laughing at everything. Two of the stalls were already booked, giggles and whispers rising over the doors. They shut themselves into a third, leaned against opposite walls. Rita watched her finger out a vial from her jeans pocket, a tiny spoon attached to the inside of the cap. They each did four hits. The coke fuel-injected Rita's heart, tripped her into serious mode. She thought she might actually want to do Dee. Not because she was beautiful, but because she had a wildness in her, a thing wanting to get out. It had flashed out of her on the dance floor, erratic, a pure light channeled crazily through a fractured diamond. Rita remembered how it was when her own thing had been set free. Glory days. Nights of divine madness.

"You're an actress, too," Rita said. "Right?"

Dee was still breathing hard from the dancing. She caught a drain, swallowed. "How'd you know?"

Rita pointed to her brain. "We sense these things. You worked any?"

"I did some modeling when I was younger. But I didn't like it. Now I'm in Theater Arts down at Berkeley."

"I'll give you my number in LA before I leave. If you want, I can introduce you to some people."

"That'd be awesome! Thank you!"

"With your looks," Rita said, "couple years I might be thanking you for givin' me a crumb from your table."

A silence slid in between them. Rita read some of the graffiti. To the right of Dee's head were eight felt-tip representations of a hand with its thumb and forefinger held apart, measuring distances ranging from miniscule to small. Under each drawing was the name of a man. Marty Kass. Jack Sauter. Clay Homanski. Someone had gone to great pains.

"You're an amazing dancer," Dee said shyly. "Really amazing."

"I was inspired." Rita reached out, caressed her cheek, and Dee rubbed against her palm.

"No." Dee peeled Rita's hand from her cheek, kissed it, then let it fall, only the fingers touching. "You're so alive. You're the most alive person here. I saw it when you were walking toward us. It wasn't how you moved, it was just who you are. Everyone was staring."

"A female skunk would draw stares in this crowd."

Dee's manner was all naive fire and sincerity. "Don't put yourself down! You're so beautiful!"

Rita honeyed up her voice. "I'm not the one's beautiful here."

The girl's mouth shaped itself into a pout. "I've got a face...but there's nothing behind it. I'm ordinary."

"How you figure?"

"When I look at myself...it's just a face."

"You can't see nothing in a mirror." Rita laid a finger beside her right eye. "This here's where you wanna look."

Keeping her back to the wall, Dee tilted her head toward Rita, and there it was again, that flash from inside, a ray of gemmy brilliance sawing wildly out, like a klieg light gone off its moorings.

"What do you see?" she asked.

"I see myself," said Rita.

The answer appeared to stop Dee, to cut her juice for a second. Then she said, "Don't lie to me," in a damaged voice.

Rita caught up her hand. "That's what I see. Myself without all the healed-up places, all the shit of life." She played with the girl's fingers. "I see an actress waiting for the right part."

A change in Dee's face, as if the wild thing was eased and had withdrawn, leaving her a girl again. Anxious. Innocent and smitten.

"Did you come with Janine?" Rita asked.

"Yeah, but..." Dee blushed. "But...uh..."

"You're not together?"

"No." Dee shook her head with solemnity, as if she knew this to be a step taken.

A toilet flushed; somebody said, "Oh, shit."

Rita stroked the inside of Dee's wrist with her thumb. "I wanna kiss you again," she said. She moved close, and Dee looped both arms about her neck. A stall door banged, and two girls shrieked laughter, the sound reverberating in the tiled space. Dee tensed, but relaxed when Rita sipped freshness from her mouth. Tequila and toothpaste. Rita liked the way Dee took control of the kiss, aggressive with her tongue, the wild thing starting to slither free. Dee pushed her gently away, slipped off her T-shirt. Her breasts were milky white, largish and high, the engorged pink nipples like mints on hotel pillows. Rita cupped them, hefted them, squeezed them together so she could serpent-kiss both nipples at once. Dee whispered, "Oh god...." Fingers tangled in Rita's hair.

"Now you!" Dee said urgently. "I want to see you."

Rita straightened. She rolled a nipple between her fingers, gave it a pinch to regain control. "Don't rush it," she said. "Something this sweet, you let it simmer till the flavor's strong."

Jimmy located a spot where he could pull the van into the bushes off the road leading to Major Borchard's compound, just past the abandoned shack with the target tacked to one collapsed wall. He cut the engine, climbed cautiously out, watching where he stepped. Dry leaves crackled underfoot, fallen twigs clawed his bootheels. He walked back along the road to the shack, using a flashlight to point the way, then pushed through thick brush until he was standing by the steps. Rotten-looking boards. He gave them a kick to see if anything scurried away, tested them to learn if they would bear his weight, and shined the flashlight underneath them. He probed the skewed doorway with the light, illuminating yellowed magazines, a broken chair, an empty cartridge box from which the printing and color had been scrubbed by the weather. An old smell of decomposition, almost subsumed by the resiny scent of spruce, issued from within. Satisfied by the absence of pests, he sat himself down. The board step was damp and creaked beneath him. At his back, the ruin seemed to release a faint moldy breath. He wondered how the shack had served Major Borchard. Maybe a place of initiation. Send a racist cub down to sit in it until he had visions of Ivory Joe Jesus or the town of Maumbad Heiglitz where Hitler got his first woody. Might be it was holy ground, the primitive shelter where Bob Champion, possessed by the spirit of Liberty, had come to plan his sacred bank robberies and write his irresistible screed. Or maybe the shack was pre-Borchard, being the ancestral home of the elusive and terrible Caucasaurus, the progenitor of those noble savages whose cave paintings of lynchings and burning crosses could still be found in sewer tunnels beneath certain land-grant universities in the South. The more he talked to Borchard, the more Jimmy thought the major had been snagged by his own hook, reeled himself in, and was now preparing to mount his own stiffening body on a trophy plaque. His claim of being the exemplar of a philosophy purified of any taint of racism…What a hoot! Borchard had lost contact with his true imperatives. He was like a man who thought he could reach the Heavenly City by swallowing a Bible, and having done so, had proceeded to shit out the best parts, the parts he most believed in…It started to rain. Drops splatted on the roof, but the canopy was so thick overhead, Jimmy scarcely felt a one. He listened to the dark. Apart from the rain, there was only the distant humming of the expressway, a streak of sound that seemed to run alongside the rest of reality, measuring some fundamental quality, like the bar registering the levels of a soundtrack beside a frame of raw film. He supposed he should go on up to the house and give the major the bad news, but he didn't feel like dealing with him just yet.

The story tugged at him, trying to drag him under its surface, but he wasn't ready to go there. It had taken an unplanned turning, and though this had been true of other stories, it never was easy to accept. It felt like a hand had reached in from somewhere and reconfigured his characters. The way he'd laid it out, Susan and Aaron would run off together, and the narrative would have eased to conclusion. Not every loose thread would get tied, but that was how he wanted it to be. Like life. Sloppy and unpredictable. Now that Susan had rejected Aaron, things were going to play out badly for everyone. Having used her cousin, manipulated him with her flesh, how could she wash that stain from her soul? The last of her innocence spent, she'd follow a cynic's road to hell, engaging in desultory affairs, trying to recapture something she would never have lost if she'd obeyed the rule of her nature, and ultimately would sink into depravity, into foulness of every description, becoming herself the thing she had hated. And Aaron...it was over for him. Hope crushed; love destroyed; stumbling in tears away from Susan's bedroom. What other end could he pursue apart from that to which he had been turned? How else exorcise rage and frustration than by confronting the monster who had transformed his cousin's sweetness into perfidy? That was how he viewed it. Susan's ardor had seemed of unalloyed quality, yet she could not of a sudden have abandoned their involvement unless the involvement itself were false, unless she were false. All her complaints about the colonel, her suggestion that if she were free of him, unmarried, then she and Aaron might further explore the attraction between them — they had been tools with which to shape his rage. Recognizing this, it might

123

be assumed that he would resist such usage, but seeing how she had been molded into this duplicitous form goaded him into a fury whose force went beyond what even Susan might have hoped, all of it directed at the man who had murdered her heart.

Anger armored his thoughts against the process of reason, and he drove his right fist into a door that, by chance, he happened to be passing. The door, which had not been completely closed, swung inward, and, shaking his hand in pain, he gazed into what appeared to be the colonel's sitting room, a carpeted space furnished with sturdy chairs and a leather sofa and a massive desk. Military memorabilia on the walls. Aaron thought it most ordinary to be the den of such a malignant beast. But upon entering and lighting a lamp, after walking about and touching the room's contents, he gained a profound sense of the colonel's vileness. The man's essence clung to his belongings. It was in the shine of the several pairs of boots arranged as though on regimental display in the closet; in the alphabetized dispatches occupying various files; in the gilt-framed painting of an eagle rendered in a style apparently intended to portray the bird's majesty and ferocity, but that had in its excess succeeded rather in portraying it as mad and ludicrously proud; in the loops and flourishes of the florid signature affixed to documents on the desk; in the cold gleam of the holstered sidearm now doing duty as a paperweight. Afflicted by these and other glimmers of the colonel's gross spirit, flooded with hatred, Aaron slumped into the chair beside the desk and, acting from a stance of less purposeful inspection than perverse curiosity, began to examine Colonel Rutherford's papers. Letters, dispatches, orders, government contracts — nothing caught his interest until he came upon a letter posted a week earlier from an address in Matanzas informing the colonel that his lodge was ready for occupancy. Aaron pocketed this letter. He sat without moving for a considerable time, his thoughts running a tedious and unproductive circuit, ranging from intent to determination to the desire to flee Havana, to travel somewhere beyond the influence of his beautiful cousin, if such a destination existed anywhere on earth. But each stop on the circuit directed him onward to the next, and he came to understand that thinking would afford him no escape. He slipped the gun, a Colt of recent vintage, from the holster. It, too, he pocketed. When he stood, the weight of the gun caused him to feel overbalanced, as if his flesh and bones were by comparison insubstantial.

Instead of going immediately to the front door, as he had commanded himself to do, he returned to Susan's door, pausing before it. Her light remained on, yet he detected no sound from within. He had presumed that she would be weeping, perhaps not for the same reasons he had wept, but expressive of some feeling at least akin to his own. The silence made him wonder if she had injured herself, or if she might have fallen into a dangerous fugue, one prompted by emotional conflict. He thought to investigate for the sake of her well being, but then recognized that he was merely attempting to justify having a last glimpse of her. He wrenched himself from the door and hurried down the stairs and then sprinted out onto the grounds, in his anguish moving away from the house but not along the driveway that led to the gate. Within a matter of seconds, he became disoriented, lost in a darkness of palms, a space thick with shrubs bearing large blooms lent a sickly white luster by angling shafts of moonlight. He saw the lights of the house behind him, but could find no sign of a path. Pushing aside branches, he forced a path through the shrubbery, emerging at the rear of the house, beside the trunk of a tree with an enormous spreading crown. A window on the second floor, one overlooking a sapling palm, had been thrown open, and Susan was standing in it, her filmy nightdress molded to her by the breeze, much of her comely shape revealed. Aaron's emotions upon seeing her were too complex to be summed up by a single word or even several, though a sickly yearning colored the surface of his feelings. He approached the window and when she saw him, he withdrew the Colt from his pocket and brandished it aloft.

"This is what you want?" he shouted. "This?"

She said nothing. Her face appeared in repose.

"For God's sake, Susan!" Aaron lowered his arm and let the gun dangle at his side. For a long interval he was unable to speak. Finally, in calmer voice, he said, "Susan, come with me. Please! We can catch the morning boat."

She maintained her silent pose, and Aaron had the urge, both formed and fully imagined in an instant, to fire at her, watch her fall, and then turn the weapon on himself. But his urge did not translate into action. His fingers had grown as cold and inflexible as the Colt itself.

"Will you not speak to me?" Tears came into his eyes and he pressed the heel of his free hand to his brow, trying to restrain them.

Her voice drifted down to him, seeming — despite the character of her words — pitiless, devoid of feeling. "I'm sorry, Aaron. I don't know what to say."

He looked up to her again, saw nothing familiar, no cousin to whom he might appeal on grounds of history or natural affection, only the figure of a beautiful woman, smiling, yet of an aspect one could only describe in terms of ferocity, posed like the Helen of her age, gazing at a sight she alone could envision, a conflagration whose every particular she was happy to have inspired. He could not bear to her see so. He turned and walked unsteadily off along the drive, unable to think of an immediate destination, a new heaviness in his chest. Outside the gate, he stopped and looked about. His eyes were blurred. He heard a noise that, when he glanced up at the trembling bright signals in the sky, he imagined to be the stars rattling in their dice cups. Seconds later, a hansom drawn by two blinkered roans, the driver's face obscured by a wide-brimmed hat, hurtled past with a shattering noise. Lights veered at him, and the outlines of trees and street and houses shifted about like jackstraws, assembling the likeness of a grotesque netherworld where shadows watched from the triangular windows of spindly towers and huge impaled spiders waved their legs atop long curving pins. Even after his eyes had cleared, he recognized nothing of the night.

Dee was enraptured by Rita's tattoo. She kissed each scale of the snake and licked the apple shiny. Then she pressed herself against Rita, going breast to breast. She put her mouth to Rita's ear, fingered her belt buckle, and whispered, "I want to go down on you." Rita inhaled the mango-rinse cigarette-smoke smell of her hair, slid her breasts back and forth against Dee. This perfect, tit-slippery, ice-cream girl, all soft and de-siring, kneeling on the floor of the john and getting wet-faced between her thighs....The picture fit an empty frame in Rita's album.

"Baby," she said. "You go ahead do what you want."

Dee worked her jeans and panties down, so Rita could free up her right leg and plant a foot atop the toilet. The women in the other stalls weren't talking now, maybe listen-ing for sex...maybe having sex themselves. Music filtered in from another world, ponderous and bass-heavy. Dee's tongue put a charge into Rita, and Rita restrained her with the heel of her hand. "Go easy, baby," she said. "Take your sweet time." But Dee wasn't hearing her. She was all over Rita's pussy, into every fold, like a hungry cat in a hurry to catch all of a spill, short on technique but her enthusiasm was way off the scale, and Rita told herself to hell with lessons, let's ride this honey train. She thought she heard the crackling of a fire in her mind, a sigh that might have been hers, and then her singularity of focus was washed away by a million thoughts, observations, urgencies, each surfacing from oblivion and scrapping to be number one, none of them sus-tained. The bathroom door swung open, admitting a gust of guitar drums screams, and then swung closed, sealing out the beast. Water ran, women chattered, the door opened and closed again. Rita was carried beyond it all. Orgasm slapped her back against the cold metal wall, then bent her nearly double and left her hugging Dee's head, which was turned to the side, eyes closed. Rita felt stuck in the moment, as if the air in the stall had hardened into a Lucite block entrapping them. She was happy there, happy for innocence and wildness, happy to be hugging this girl whom she believed she could change. From another stall came a sardonic, southern voice: "Ya'll try not to hurt yourself over there!"

Giggles.

Rita urged Dee to her feet. "Baby," she said. "You mind if I take you outa here?"

Big-eyed and pale, like what she'd done had scared her, Dee said, "Uh-huh."

"Okay." Rita yanked on her panties and jeans.

The bathroom door opened, clattery footsteps, and then an alarmed cry: "Dee!"

Under her breath Dee said with exasperation, "Oh, Christ!"

Rita finished buckling her belt. Somebody pounded on a stall door. "Fuck off!" said the southern girl.

A third woman said, impatiently, "She's not here, Janine."

Rita thought she recognized BJ's voice. She opened the door. Janine was leaning against one of the sinks, looking fat and pitiful, hair mussed, a damp splotch mapping her blouse like a dark continent on a plaid sea. The fluorescents painted her ghastly pale. She stared off behind Rita, to where Dee was holding up the T-shirt to cover her breasts. Standing to the right of Janine, BJ touched a hand to her forehead and said to Rita in an aggravated tone, "Did you have to open the fucking door?"

Rita stepped clear of the stall. "What's the problem?"

Janine made a glutinous noise, as if to spit, and staggered a little. Tears crystalled her eyes, then flowed.

"Let's go," said BJ, tugging at her arm as Dee came out of the stall, fully dressed now.

A *guk-guk* sound, a hiccup, issued from Janine's throat.

"Come on!" said BJ.

Janine shook her off, petulance uglying up her face. "Cunt," she said thickly to Denise. "Fucking cunt…slut."

"You left out 'bitch,'" said Rita.

The blond's eyes skipped to her. "You….you're the bitch." She said it without much conviction, as if she had only just noticed and had not yet processed all the evidence.

A stall door closer to the exit flew open, and three girls emerged. "'Scuse us," one said, hand-signaling apology. "Just passing through."

They fled into the din.

Rita turned to tell Dee they should leave, and the blond rushed her, a mushy weight slamming her into a partition. Rita braced, grabbed a handful of half-tit, half-blouse, wrenched and spun the blond into a stall and pinned her against the wall with an elbow barred under the chin. A scream from BJ. The blond's blue eyes went buggy. She clawed ineffectually at Rita. Slobber filmed over her chin. A few ounces more pressure, Rita thought, and it would be thumbs down for this first-time gladiator. Her heart, speedy from the coke, had slowed. The skin of her face felt cold, bloodless.

"Don't hurt her!" Dee laid a hand on Rita's shoulder. "Please!"

Rita slung the blond about, shoved her down onto the toilet. She sat with knees spread, holding her throat and gagging.

Dee pulled Rita away, then toward the exit. "Let me talk to her."

"You start talking to her," Rita said, "and we might as well say our good-byes right now."

"That's not true." Dee kissed her. "I'll be out soon as I can. Wait for me?"

"All right," Rita said offhandedly.

Dee rested her arms on Rita's shoulders. "You don't believe me?"

"If you say so."

"Do you know what you are?" The girl enveloped Rita in a hug and whispered. "You couldn't! If you did, you'd know I *have* to be with you."

Her intensity touched off Rita's paranoia, but she had already decided to disregard such signs. "I believe you," she said.

"It might take a while, but I promise I'll be there." Another kiss. "Promise you'll wait?"

"Yeah, I'll wait. I might be in the parking lot. If not, I'll be at the bar."

Rita passed back into the club, BJ at her heels. The band was on another break, and the jukebox was down so low, the song it played was all but drowned in a surflike babble. People milled on the dance floor. Shouts demanding music arose. Rita felt the ruler of all she saw.

"That was some shit," said BJ. She had a furtive, skittish look, touching her hair, shifting her weight from foot to foot. "Janine's been crazy 'bout Dee for fucking ever. And Dee knows it...."

"Not my business," Rita said, cutting in.

"If you're getting involved with Dee, you might want..."

"We ain't talking about a lifelong relationship here." Rita angled her head an inch toward BJ. "You got a cigarette."

"I don't smoke." A few seconds pissed themselves away, then the blow-job queen said, "I thought you were interested in Walter."

"'Interested' ain't quite the word."

"Well, if you *are,* you should watch yourself. He's hard on his girlfriends. I hear he gets physical with them sometimes."

Rita scouted the crowd, not searching for anyone in particular, just looking for potential.

"Friend of mine says he beat her up," said BJ by way of clarification.

"It'll happen," Rita said.

"Y'know…" BJ let it slide, then fired up again. "I don't know what you're after, but Walter and Dee, they both have issues. Dee's impressionable, and a little crazy, I think."

"Maybe she and Walt should get together."

"Don't think he hasn't tried!"

The band came back onto the stage, picking up guitars. The drummer did rim shots, rolled the snare, rattling his cage.

"I'm just concerned." BJ put hands on hips. "I don't want to see Dee get hurt."

"You're lucky, you'll be somewhere else when she does," said Rita.

"That's a great attitude!"

Rita gave her full attention, lashing out. "Who are you? Her troop leader?"

BJ stood up bravely. "I'm her friend."

"You're such a friend, whyn't you come on back to the room with us and referee? That way you can make sure she don't get hurt. Hell, you can even join in the fun. I'm liberal that way." Rita went jaw-to-jaw with her. "That don't do it for ya, I'd advise you to keep the bullshit to yourself, 'cause I'm sick of hearing your mouth work."

Unbowed, BJ held her ground.

Rita chested her, knocking her back a foot. "You got something else to say?"

BJ pretended to cower. "Hey, do who the fuck you want! I don't care."

"It's the best way to be," said Rita.

Aaron had never associated evergreens with Cuba, but the road to the colonel's lodge traveled not through the lush vegetation typical of the lowlands, but wound through towering, dark green sentinels, rank upon rank of them, such as you might find in the pristine forests of the Northwest. The air was crisp, and he shivered as he walked — he had brought no clothes suitable for the heights of Matanzas. With a trace of desperate glee, he thought that had he anticipated this side trip, he might have packed his tweed jacket, though it was far too dignified a garment for the errand he had been designated to perform.

The road terminated at a gate surmounted by a sign on which had been painted a rampant red-eyed stag. Whether figment of the colonel's ego or element of his family coat of arms, either way it spoke to the man's unnatural degree of arrogance. The gate, a construction of planks and wire, was locked. Beyond it, the road dwindled to a path that wound away into the trees at a sharp incline. Aaron thought he made out a light through the boughs, but doubted anyone would hear if he were to call out. He searched along the fence for a means of ingress. Finding none, he was on the verge of attempting to scale it, when a man hailed him, saying, "Get your ass away from the fence!"

The man, whom Aaron assumed to be the colonel's servant, was a roosterish little fellow distinguished by a head of close-cropped whitish blond hair, and further by the rifle of peculiar design that he was aiming at Aaron's chest. "Oh, it's you," he said. "You bring it?"

The question forced Aaron to make yet another assumption—that the man had mistaken him for someone else. "I brought it," he said.

"Awright!" The servant ported his rifle. "The man's gonna love your shit."

He led Aaron back to the gate, fumbled with a ring that must have held several dozen keys. He cocked an eye toward Aaron. "So how about you show it to me?"

"I beg your pardon," Aaron said, uncertain what to do.

"You take some stupid pills?" The servant squinted at him, and sucked on his upper lip, a gesture that caused his mouth, which was extremely small and delicate by contrast to the rest of his loutish features, nearly to disappear. "The gun! You said you brought it."

Should the servant have knowledge of the weapon in question, Aaron realized that he might then be forced to shoot him, an option he did not want to elect—the noise might alert the colonel. But not to produce the gun seemed an even less attractive option. Tentatively, Aaron drew the Colt from his jacket pocket. The servant inspected it.

"That's it?" said the servant. "That's Bob Champion's gun?"

Aaron could conceive of no reason to not to say, as he then did, "Yes."

"Way Ray was going on, I figured it'd be gold-plated."

Without first asking for permission, the servant seized the Colt by its barrel and wrenched it from Aaron's hand. He thereupon took a crouching position and pretended to fire at, presumably, imaginary targets hidden among the trees, making spit-filled explosive noises to simulate the sound of fire. He winked at Aaron and said, "Guess I killed them niggers."

"I don't believe the colonel will appreciate your delaying me with this frivolity," Aaron said. "If you insist on delaying me further, I will be forced to report your behavior."

"Hell's wrong with you?" The servant edged away. "You on something?"

"Please hand me the weapon. Or shall I return to town and report a theft to the authorities?"

"I don't know I should let you in. You sound like you on something."

"The only thing I'm 'on' is an errand to deliver this gun to your master." Aaron held out his hand. "Now give it to me."

Grudgingly, the servant tossed the Colt to Aaron and turned again to the lock. "I'm gonna keep an eye on you— you ain't acting normal." He swung open the gate and performed a mocking bow.

As they negotiated the rocky path toward the lodge, the servant continued to harass Aaron, suggesting in no uncertain terms that he might be prone to a number of debilitating conditions. "I didn't think much of you, you was out last time," he said. "But least you acted like a human being, not like some kinda faggot. That's it, ain't it? You a goddamn fairy. AIDs is crawling up your asshole."

These nonsequiturs did not perturb Aaron. On passing inside the compound, a sense of calm had settled over him. He felt grounded in — indeed, comforted by — the inevitability of what was soon to happen. Though thoughts of Susan assaulted him still and his heart hung heavy in his chest, those things were counterweighted by a cold emergent anger attaching to the realization that within a short while he would look into Colonel Rutherford's eyes for the last time. It would be interesting to see what lay there.

Melting up from the shadows, its every window lit, the lodge was more impressive a structure than Susan's sketchy description had led Aaron to believe. Large and appropriately rustic in design, with a wide porch columned by logs, set about with hand-hewn chairs. Viewed from the path below, fortified by massive boulders and guarded by towering sentries, it seemed both splendid and pagan, a sentient production of the forest floor, the genius of the place given over to the form of a squarish, many-eyed head made of logs and pitch, glowing furnace-bright with inner fire, whose brute body was nine-tenths buried in the earth.

At the foot of the steps, the servant placed a restraining hand on Aaron's chest and said, "Major's working in his study. I'm gonna leave you downstairs, but don't you go poking around. Don't touch nothing! We straight on that?"

"As you wish."

Could the man be ignorant of his master's rank? Scornfully, Aaron thought that the colonel's choice of servants offered a pungent comment on all his judgments, the clumsiest being the one he had made concerning his wife's character. But then not even Aaron had suspected that Susan's graceful form embraced such a depth of rage and iniquity. As the servant turned to mount the steps, Aaron struck him behind the ear with the butt of the Colt — he had no complaint against the fellow, but left to his own devices, he might prove a threat. The servant slumped to his hands and knees, groaning, and

Aaron struck again, laying him out flat. He then proceeded to lift the man onto his shoulder, a chore of no small difficulty, and carried him up the steps and into a long, well-appointed room lit by several lamps and by a fire roaring in a hearth so grand, it would have been sufficient to warm a castle keep. He deposited the servant on a leather couch and hunted about for something with which to bind him. Unable to find rope, he switched off the lamps and stripped them of their cords, making certain he had enough left over to bind the colonel. Protruding from the servant's jacket pocket was a bandana, and this Aaron used for a gag. Once he had completed his task, holding the Colt in his right hand, he took a chair in the shadows to the side the hearth, so that he would be hidden from the view of anyone descending the stair at the far end of the room.

Gazing into the hearth settled Aaron's pulse, which his act of violence had elevated to an alarming rate. In the flames that flourished behind an ironwork screen, among the ember-edged logs, gone to charred blackness in patches, he saw the fall of a great city, its toppled towers trapping a defeated citizenry who, burning yet alive, skittered helter-skelter amid the blazing ruin of their culture. Watching them scamper, he imagined himself as God might perceive him: a tiny creature with a relatively clean soul who, moved by a single debasing flaw that ran through the center of his being like the dark twist at the heart of a ruby, was preparing to commit murder. He cursed Susan, not for what she had done, but for the fact of her existence, and he cursed God, too, for having created of his, Aaron's, own blood the only woman whom he could love. In face of such sacrilege, a man of the cloth might cite God's mysterious ways, or suggest that it was not given us to know all things. But there was no mystery here. No deep philosophical conundrum. Either God in his boredom, perceiving the earth to be a dwindling concern, had relaxed his moral regulations so as to create a more entertaining prospect, or else — and this was the bitter regulation Aaron now accepted — the tablets with which Moses had returned from the mountaintop were either a misreading or a conscious manipulation of the one true commandment, Do What Thou Wilt and Suffer.

Logs shifted in the fire, the city's fall complete, and Aaron, too, fell, collapsed, surrendered to the pressures that bound him to that place and time. He had a sudden apprehension of his position. Alone and friendless in a strange land; about to dare the wrath of god and, more pertinently, that of all the powerful men who had a vested interest in the life of Colonel Rutherford; too weak to escape the prison of his compulsions. How the thought of Cuba had changed for him! No longer a paradise isle, a postcard panorama of beaches and brown bodies, but a territory of darkness and flame that even now might be marshalling its forces against him, summoning spirits from the wild. Impious policemen with gold teeth and red hands and black guns, old luminous saints, and licorice-skinned demons of the talking drum...The servant stirred, moaned, and Aaron, whose attention had been so enlisted by his imagination that he had forgotten the man, started from his chair, panicked and uncertain. He went to the sofa to inspect his victim. The man's face was pale. In the flickering light, the beads of sweat on his brow shimmered like crystals. A considerable patch of his whitish hair was matted with blood, and the blood had trickled down into the creases of his neck, drying there in tributary patterns. His right eye was partially open — firelight made the slit glow orange and silver, the colors gliding along the surface of the humor, as if it were composed not of human stuff but some rare infernal element. He moaned again. Aaron leaned over him, resting a knee on the sofa, intending to give him another tap with the Colt to keep him quiet, but as he drew back his arm, the lightning of impulse galvanized his muscles, tensing him throughout, and recognizing that the man could not survive, must not survive, he brought his arm down in what he knew might prove a killing stroke.

✦

On her way out of Gainer's, Rita bummed a cigarette from a bouncer. She smoked it off at the edge of the lot, at the end of the row of cars closest to the highway, leaning on the hood of a vintage Buick with a rain-beaded windshield and a grille like a toothy chrome fish mouth. It was her first cigarette in months, and it made her dizzy. She slid up onto the wet fender of the Buick and crossed her legs. From this distance the music sounded like derangement — guitar squeals breaking free from pulsing bass walls, now and then a fragment of shouted vocal. The fools by the front door were shoving each other, yelling, gearing up for a fight. Beyond the lot lay a vast acreage of brush-covered fields, some strung with surveyor's twine, the future homes of Mr. Goodwrench and Krispy Kreme. To the west, the riverine brightness of the expressway. The sky was all low clouds that reflected a dusky orangeness of metropolitan Seattle. Up near the light poles she could see a fine rain falling, but by the time it hit her hair, she could scarcely feel it. Rita blew smoke rings, watched the coils grow shapeless in the mist. She wondered what Jimmy was up to. Wasn't much point to worrying about him. She could feel the circuit that channeled energy between them glowing white hot, hotter than it had ever been, and from that she understood that he was writing the finish to their story. And it was *their* story now that she had manipulated him to change the ending, but she wasn't sure he would carry it through. She wasn't sure she wanted him to. If he did, whatever happened, she'd be in the clear, but she was not prepared to lose him. Not until she was ready to take the step she had programmed him to take, and she realized that she was not ready…though the energy of the story was hard to resist, inspiring her to go with the flow, to surrender to the impulses it generated.

Maybe she was ready.

She flicked the cigarette butt out into the road, exhaled a final stream of smoke, and thought about Dee. That angel had a couple of loose wires, for real, but Rita sure did admire the way they sparked. Crazy goes to college. She bet the Berkeley Theater Arts department had their hands full with sweet Denise. She probably put on a hell of a show whenever they asked her to do a sense memory exercise. Who could have put that crack in her? Daddy, maybe…

Rita noticed a blond guy in a red shirt crossing the lot toward her. Walter's friend. "Hi," he said as he ambled up. "Walter's looking for you."

"He must be looking in the wrong places."

"Want me to tell him where you are?"

"That's what you want."

This stumped him. He hovered, betwixt and between. He had, she saw, a good face. A little fleshy, but sound. A solid fundamental person. She wondered what he was doing hanging out with Walter.

"You really an actress?" he asked.

"Can't you tell?"

"Not really." He laughed appreciatively. "I guess that means you are. You're good-looking enough, for sure."

"I forget your name," Rita said.

"Miles…Miles Ludwig."

She imagined a ludwig, a khaki German bug goose-stepping on eight legs, carrying eight shiny rifles.

"Junior," he added. "My dad's the Miles Ludwig Motors guy. Maybe you caught his commercials? Every other word he says is 'miles.'" He affected, presumably, his dad's bombastic delivery. "'We're miles ahead in low prices, miles ahead in value, with miles and miles and miles of cars…'"

"That what you do?" she asked. "You work for your daddy?"

"For now. I'm thinking about going back to grad school next year." He shoved his hands into his pockets, drew a line in the dirt with the point of his loafer. "So what happened in the bathroom?"

"You're old enough to figure that out."

Nonplussed, he said, "Maggie said something happened in the bathroom with you and Janine and Dee."

"Maggie?"

"You were sitting next to her in the bar."

"The blow-job queen," said Rita.

"Wha-at?" Miles sort of laughed the word.

"I forgot her name. Probably not an accurate description."

"Well, actually…" Miles laughed again.

Rita poked his arm. "Miles! You dog!"

"Hey, she never did it with me! I wasn't saying that."

Rita scowled. "Why would I give a damn she sucked your dick? You think I believe oral sex is an impropriety?"

"Sorry," he said.

A biker roared into the parking lot, sat gunning his engine in front of the entrance, checking things out. The fools by the door gave him a wide berth. When he left they resumed their pushing and shouting.

"Fucking bikers," said Miles, and then, as if those words had been intelligence enough, he fell silent. With forced animation, he asked, "You ever work on a picture with bikers in it? Y'know…like as extras?"

"This the reason you're out here with me, Miles?" she asked in a syrupy voice. "To ask questions, to learn my opinion on various subjects?"

"No," he said defensively. Then he caught her meaning and said, "No, I…I wanted to talk to you."

"*Talk* to me?"

"Yeah," he said, getting bashful. "Y'know."

"That's what you been doing is it? Talking?"

Miles was at a loss.

"Whyn't you come a little closer?" Rita patted the fender. "I bet you can talk a whole lot better over here."

She spread her knees so he could walk up between them, push himself against her. He went at it like he loved her. Careful with her mouth. Tasting the corners. Taking the tour before he stuck in his tongue. His dick fattened against her thigh. Miles, she thought. Good dog, good lad. When he broke for air, he appeared to be searching for something to say. A compliment, a suggestion as to change of venue. She pulled him back into a kiss. One hand squeezed her ass, another timidly settled on a breast. She writhed against him, a pretense. Dee had a better style, though she liked the hungriness that swept over Miles each time she responded...Then a furious yell and somebody ploughed into them. Rita toppled off the fender, landing on her belly. The fall took her wind. More yelling. Sounds of struggle. Gasping, she got herself turned and saw Walter standing over Miles, who was on his knees. Walter had him by the shirtfront and was punching down into his bloody face. Each blow made a flat smacking noise, and as he threw, Walter would let out a truncated scream and a spray of spittle. Miles looked to be borderline conscious, not defending himself. Rita came to her haunches, slid the hunting knife from her boot, held it hidden beneath her thigh.

"Hey, Walter!" she called sweetly.

His fist drawn back, he glanced sidelong at her. His mask had rotted way to reveal the unnatural Aryan motherfucker beneath. He released his hold. Miles sagged, slumped in the dirt. Walter squared up to Rita. His smile had gone on break. In his face was wormy loathing and the joy of violence. Blood dripped from his hand.

"Fucking Indian bitch!" he said.

"That's me." Rita eased up into a crouch, backed toward the rear of the Buick.

Walter followed, not in a hurry. He seemed to feel he was on top of the situation. "Bitch! You think you can cocktease me?"

"Didn't I already do that, Walt?" Rita turned the corner of the Buick, kept on backing, one hand on the trunk for balance. When he turned after her, she showed him the knife, edge out, ready for business.

His smile resurfaced, and she took it as a good sign. The smile, she thought, was his hedge against insanity, the place he retreated to when his confidence dimmed. "You better mean that," he said.

"Oh, I'm gonna bleed ya, Walt. Don't you worry. You just keep coming."

He braced, legs wide. She could tell he was expecting it low…if he expected it at all. His knees were stiff, his torso canted forward. Bad move, Walt.

"Well, do it," he said, his voice amped with repressed laughter.

"Please," she said, whining, lowering the knife a little. "Please…just go away!"

He relaxed the slightest bit, the tension leaving his shoulders, and she slashed at his eyes. His weight was set all wrong, and when he tried to twist away, his heel caught and he went sprawling onto his back, falling behind the car parked beside the Buick. Before he could recover, she had straddled him, her knees pinning his arms and shoulders, back hunched to lower her center of gravity, the knife poised above his right eye.

"One twitch," she said, "they be calling you Patch."

He stared at the knife as if seeing God.

"Oh-oh!" she said blithely. "Guess you fucked up, huh?"

He licked his lips, said, "…unh…"

She cocked an ear. "Say again."

"Don't…" he said.

A groan from the front of the Buick. Sounded like the groaner was in miles and miles of pain.

"You did a job on your friend," Rita said. "What was on your mind, Walt? What caused your outrage? Surely you didn't think I was gonna fuck you?"

A car passed on the road, headlights flashing over them. His eyes tracked after it.

"No hope there, man," she said. "They saw us at all, they probably think you just giving me some sugar. And nobody can see us from the bar, so we got all kindsa time. We can get to know each other."

She felt him tensing, brought the point of the knife closer to his eye, and said, "Relax."

More groaning.

"I don't believe you gonna be getting a sweetheart deal at Ludwig Motors anytime soon." Rita edged up higher on his chest, her crotch tight to his chin. "I know why you kicked his ass. 'Cause you could. I can relate to that."

His glare weakened, and Rita could see inside him. The fear, the razors that had reshaped his reason. The mechanics of his stop-and-go cycle, the on buttons and off switches. Boy was damn near crazy mean enough to be a senator. They saw the same things, but from different angles. He was God's invention, or maybe his parents', but she had come to her notion of the world through cold experience. What in him was madness, chaos, the erratic, was in her the product of a simple decision. He had nothing to tell her, but she had a few words for him.

"Anger management," she said. "It'd be a real benefit to you, Walt. Teach ya to harness all that raw emotion."

He seemed to flash forward behind his eyes, the thing that was most of him scooting up to his eyeball to take a peek, then scuttling back into the dark.

"You get that anger working for ya. Like it's a little engine inside your skull. Get it fitted with gears so you can wind 'er out and back 'er down...You do that, I see great things ahead for you."

Walter, Rita realized, was not paying attention, no doubt rummaging his brain for some idiotic tactic and not listening to her words of wisdom. He was not a listener. It was the least of his crimes, but it made him worthless as a subject for instruction. She sliced a line straight across his forehead with the knife. He bucked against the pain, screeched, tried to grab her as she sprang away. She moved out of range, wiped the blade on some weeds growing behind the Buick. He rolled back and forth, holding his head and grunting. Blood spilled over his cheeks and nose.

"You ain't hurt," Rita said. "You might need some work, but you ain't hurt. I marked you is all."

He cursed her again, and threatened vengeance.

"Vengeance is easy when you don't give a shit," Rita told him. "If you do, it's damn near impossible."

"I'm going to kill you," he said with admirable venom. "I am going to fucking kill you."

"This might punch a dent in your self-esteem, but I ain't all that scared." She sheathed the knife in her boot. "Let me tell ya what's gonna happen. I'm going back inside and hook up with Dee. I want you to sit here and figure out a story about how your head got sliced. One that don't involve me. You involve me, I'll say you tried to rape me and I cut your ass. I believe Miles might just back me up on that."

His face was all over red. Hands, too. His eyes were shiny studs poking through a new kind of mask. Red clay and base metal.

"Maggie told me 'bout those girls you beat up," said Rita. "Bet they'd make good witnesses."

He wiped away blood that had pooled in the seam between his lips, his anger simmering. The mark she'd carved was straight and true. With stitches, he'd look like Frankenstein.

"Cops can't even bust me on a weapons charge," she said. "I ain't no actress, Walt. I sell guns and knives. I'm licensed to carry."

She heard voices, commotion, and peered over the roof of the car. Miles had tried to walk, gone about twenty-five feet before he collapsed. The doll people had found him and were on their knees beside him, squeaking. Rita dusted off her jeans.

"Make up a good story. A good story'll get you a long ways in life." She laughed and tapped Walter's leg with her toe. "I was you, I'd take that for my motto."

*

The fire in the great hearth dimmed, the room became a long shadow with a ball of orange light nestled at its center. Aaron slipped minute by minute from alertness, eyes fixed upon the stair, to near-stupefaction, gazing into the embers, his thoughts proceeding in a morose parade, like black riders coming on gloomy missions from the deserts that stretched beyond his mental horizon. He had no good sense of the passage of time. Hours might have elapsed since he had entered the lodge. He began to suspect that the colonel had retired for the evening, and since he had no knowledge of the layout of the second floor, he was hesitant to invade it. Then, too, the colonel might keep a weapon by his bed and wake to the creaking of a loose board. Nonetheless, Aaron did not think it wise to wait for morning. A disturbance, one that would summon the colonel to investigate—that might be the best tactic. Nothing that would alarm him overmuch. A noise that he would attribute to the bungling of his servant. He cast about for a suitable object and spotted a rack containing a number of rifles mounted on the wall of the entranceway. He crossed the room and saw that the rack was loosely affixed to the wall—it could be brought down without much effort.

Standing so near the door prompted Aaron to think that he could run out of the lodge and leave the colonel to explain the death of his servant. But he would find a way, surely, to explain it—that was no solution to the problem posed by his existence. And then there was the question of where Aaron might go. Havana? New York? He did not believe he could return to his life, his business. It was not that those things held no value to him, but rather he was about to take a step that would render them valueless, that would so transform him, he would no longer conform to the niche into which he had inserted himself, imprisoning the more turbulent aspects of his nature within an armor of serge and respectability. He had half-taken that step already, and perhaps, he thought, even half a step would be too much to retrace. He felt for an instant confused, the world of his purpose murkily defined, but then he imagined that in the glass panel of the front door he saw Susan at her window, her nightdress blowing around her like the ghost of a flame, the image of beauty and the anger that was destroying her. With a savage twist, he sent rifles and rack clattering to the floor and returned to his chair in the shadows.

Seconds later he heard footsteps overhead, a voice bellowing: "Randy!" He heard another shout, nearer to hand. Then the colonel's tread as he descended the stair. He wore a red-and-white checkered bathrobe and slippers. His beard had been shaved, leaving in place a set of mustaches and exposing a too-prominent jaw. Upon noticing the wreckage of the rack and the scattered rifles, he paused in his descent. "God damn it!" he said. He strode to the door and threw it open. "Randy!"

The sight of the colonel roused no special feeling in Aaron's breast. He must be, he thought, brimful of hate. The only change he detected in himself was a reduction in perspective from the abstract to the strategic. The colonel shouted again, listened, then with a profane outburst slammed the door and entered the room wherein Aaron was sitting. He turned the switch of a lamp. "Shit!" he said when the lamp failed to provide a light. He tried a second lamp, a third. Muttering, he went to stand in front of the hearth and warmed his hands, doubtless thinking injurious thoughts about the man who lay dead on the sofa behind him.

Cautiously, Aaron came to his feet and walked toward Colonel Rutherford, hiding the Colt behind his hip. The colonel gasped to see him and staggered to the side, his arms outflung in shock. "Jesus!" he said on recovering. "You scared the crap out of me!" Then: "What's going on? Why didn't Randy tell me you were here?"

Aaron could think of no response he wished to extend.

"Did you bring the gun?" the colonel asked.

His hand shaking slightly, Aaron aimed the Colt at the colonel's chest. "On your knees."

Disdain firmed the colonel's features. "What the hell is this?"

"On your knees!" The shout exploded from out of Aaron's lungs, as if it had been building inside him for a long time.

The colonel went stiffly to his knees; his expression retained an element of scorn. "What do you want?"

"I want you to lie down...on your face."

The colonel made no move to comply until Aaron fired above his head; then he dropped onto his belly. The bullet shattered glass in the darkness across the room, and the detonation set up a ringing in Aaron's ears. He kneeled and bound the colonel's hands behind his back with a lamp cord. A mild fragrance of bath oil arose from the man. His breath came hugely, as if from the bellows-sized lungs of a horse. Aaron urged the colonel to his feet and sat him down in a chair facing the hearth. Then he pulled a second chair around so he could himself sit and watch him. This accomplished, the object of his errand essentially achieved, he felt somewhat at loose ends. He had no desire to prolong things, but it was as if a gulf had materialized between the fortress of his intent and the army of his will. He was content to bide his time. Sooner or later, the colonel would supply him with the inspiration to act.

"I'm not alone here, you know," the colonel said.

Aaron chose not to disabuse him of the notion that help was at hand. He had withdrawn from the moment, become an observer, though he was not sure either of what had compelled him to this distance or what, in fact, he should observe. The colonel presented no great puzzle. As a specimen of mankind he was in no sense extraordinary, his character informed by a typical mixture of animal needs and human perversions. But what if this were not the case? Looking at the colonel, at the belly protruding from his bathrobe, the foolish mustaches, it was difficult to credit him with other than the most banal ration of evil; but perhaps this was a disguise, a shabby sheath enclosing a black knife of a soul. Aaron decided to question him.

146

"Why have you treated her so?" he asked, and was amazed by the soundness of his voice.

The colonel grimaced. "Oh, God! What has she been telling you now?"

"Of threats, rape, the suffocation of her spirit…no more than is your general custom."

"How many times do I have to say this? The woman is a user. A manipulator. She…"

Aaron pointed the Colt at the colonel, and he did not complete his accusation.

"I will not hear you speak against her," Aaron said. "Whatever she is, you have made her so with your maltreatment. When I knew her she was unstained in her devotion to the good."

The colonel looked with bewilderment at Aaron, then winced as he struggled to shift his bound hands to a more comfortable position. "You're not letting me defend myself," he said. "If I can't comment on what she's said about me, how do you expect me to answer your questions?"

"You misunderstand," Aaron said. "I am not asking you to offer a defense. You have no defense. I am interested in an explanation of your behavior. But if your explanation involves nothing more than an attack upon my cousin, there is no need to continue."

"Your cousin?" The colonel laughed.

"Yes, my cousin. Do you find the term inaccurate?"

"Are you telling me she's actually your cousin?" With an impassioned confusion that might have persuaded a less cynical witness than Aaron, the colonel said, "I didn't know. I…Why didn't you tell me?"

Aaron felt that to answer would be to encourage the colonel's pretense of insanity—such, he believed, was the man's intention in denying knowledge of the blood bond between Susan and himself.

His anxiety increasing, the colonel asked how could he have known, how could he have possibly known? When Aaron remained silent, the colonel railed against the silence, insisting that he be told what was happening. And when this failed to bestir Aaron, he resorted to threats. "I have friends…due any minute," he said. "They'll be armed, and I can assure you, they won't hesitate to use their weapons."

"You have no friends," Aaron told him. "Only sycophants and servants and seekers after influence. I doubt they will expend any significant effort in your salvation."

Bewilderment once again surfaced in the colonel's face, only to be replaced by a veneer of confidence. "Randy's probably lining you up right this second," he said. "He may not look like much, but he's a hell of a marksman."

"Is he?" Aaron stood and slipped the Colt into his pocket. He stepped behind Colonel Rutherford's chair and wrestled it around so the colonel could see the couch upon which his servant rested. "It seems his shooting eye is not what it once was."

The colonel took a moment to absorb the sight, then twisted his neck about so he could see Aaron's face. "What do you want?" he asked in a tone markedly less demanding than that he had used to phrase the question originally.

Aaron turned the colonel's chair back toward the hearth. "As I said. I want you to explain your treatment of my cousin."

"If you're talking about what she calls rape…" The colonel bit the end off of his sentence; then, as Aaron went to stand beside the hearth, he went on. "I…I don't think your cousin's recollection of the incident is unclouded. She's a very devout woman, and I believe she's devised a false memory to shield her from the guilt she feels—quite unnecessarily, to my mind—at having had relations outside the matrimonial bed."

"I fail to see how an affair could inhibit memory."

"We were being passionate," said the colonel. "Extremely passionate. She made a protest at one point, but then she consented. She gave me no reason to think she hadn't been party to the act."

Aaron moved the ironwork screen aside and stirred the fire with a poker that been resting in a stand beside the hearth; he set a fresh log atop the newly blazing remains.

"It's the truth...I swear!" said the colonel.

"And the threats?" asked Aaron, setting a second log in place. "Your restriction of her movements? These, too, are the result of a faulty memory?"

"I was angry. Disappointed. My God, I was in love with her! I still am! I didn't always act properly. I admit it. People are never at their best when they're in love...especially when the relationship is in trouble."

"In her letters to me, my cousin describes a life of unrelenting oppression, a husband whose insensitivity is tempered only by cruelty. Now you wish me to believe that this was all an act of the imagination? Give me some credit, sir. I'm not one of the hounds milling about your supper table, ready to pounce should a crumb fall their way. My cousin would not lie."

"Hold on!" said the colonel. "What do you mean, 'husband?'"

Aaron ignored him. The last words he had spoken had seeded him with doubt. He wondered now if everything Susan had related, and not merely the tale of her affections, could be a lie. No, it was impossible! She had been provoked to lie, steeped in the duplicitous substance of the marriage, her virtues eroded by the acids of the colonel's malignancy.

"Tell me about Carrasquel," Aaron said. "I would like to hear your justification of the act."

Dazedly, the colonel said, "What are you talking about?"

"Am I to understand you are denying knowledge of my cousin's lover? His murder?"

The colonel's manner became infected with hysteria. "What are you talking about? What in the hell is wrong with you?"

A ringing issued from another quarter of the house; the colonel glanced sharply in the direction of the sound.

"That'll be my friends," he said. "Probably calling to say they're on their way."

"In that case," Aaron said, aiming the Colt, "it might be best to conclude our interview."

"Wait," said the colonel. "No one's coming."

The ringing stopped.

"Yes," said Aaron. "But whoever called might worry that you have been injured. They might investigate." He picked up strips of lamp cord from the floor beside his chair. "I really should go."

"Listen!" said the colonel in a tone that must have quailed the women of his house. "This stuff about a lover...a murder. If she told you I was involved with that, with anything of the sort, it's just not true!"

"I'm going to tie your feet now," said Aaron. "If you thrash about or try to kick me, I will shoot you. Do you understand?"

The colonel's stare was an article of mystification. "What's going on? What's wrong with you? This is not..."

"I can shoot you now," said Aaron. "If you don't understand."

The colonel said, "I understand."

As Aaron bound the colonel's feet, he experienced a thrill of fear connected neither to the violence he was about to perpetrate, nor to any comprehensible antecedent. It seemed rather that fear itself had decided to lend a hand and was leaning in over his shoulder, a phantom mimicking his form, his movements, reminding him that he was soon to enter a sphere where many before him had traveled and few had thrived. He tucked the loose ends of the cords beneath the loops lashing the colonel's ankles and went back toward the hearth where flames were now snapping and leaping high. Seams of sap glowed molten on the fresh logs.

"Will you listen?" The colonel leaned toward Aaron, a picture of foolish entreaty, eyes wide, lips puffing. "You need to listen to me. You're making a mistake!"

"It was Susan who made the mistake." Aaron gave the fire another poke. "I am merely correcting it."

"Susan? Who's Susan?" Then the colonel shouted it: "Who in God's name is Susan?"

"Spare yourself, Colonel," Aaron said. "This is not a workable stratagem."

After a pause the colonel said, "Who do you think I am?"

Aaron continued to poke at the fire. The heat from the hearth stung his face, yet his bones were cored with ice. The bed of embers brightened and faded, drawing his eye with a hypnotic rhythm.

"It's major," said the colonel. "Major. Raymond. Borchard. That's who I am. My name. Who do you think I am?"

"How modest of you to give yourself a demotion! I wouldn't have expected such self-effacement." He turned to the colonel. "Who do I think you are? I think you're a monster of the most ordinary, yet the most dangerous variety. One incapable of perceiving his own monstrous nature."

"Try to listen to me. All right? Try to understand me." The colonel edged forward in his chair and spoke with extreme deliberation. "Something's wrong with you. The way you're talking, these names...You're not responding to what I'm saying! You may be having some kind of episode!"

Aaron laughed. "My cousin is a liar, and I'm...What? Deluded? Demented? These are tactics unworthy of an Academy graduate."

"I didn't attend the Academy!" said the colonel excitedly. "I was at the Citadel! Don't you see? I'm not who you think!"

"You know nothing of Susan? Nothing of her family, the Lisles of Buckingham? Of Aaron, her cousin?"

"No," said the colonel dully; then, louder: "No!"

"Yet earlier tonight, you recognized me, did you not?"

If the colonel's hands had been free, Aaron thought, he would have clapped them to his head in frustration, unable to counter this argument. He threw himself about in the chair, grunting and fuming. "You're fucking out of your mind!" he said.

10

A voice, not the colonel's, though it was saying much the same thing, commanded Aaron's attention. It seemed to be issuing from within him, perhaps the voice of conscience or that of a wise shadow prompting him from the wings of consciousness, urging him to break from the character of this little drama and recognize the wrongness of his part. The voice, or rather its owner, pressed forward, and Aaron felt a winnowing, an imminent dissolution that threatened to wash him away. He heard himself say, "I just want you to leave her alone," speaking in a yokel accent that was altogether different from his usual cultivated tone.

"I will!" the colonel said eagerly. "I swear before God, I will leave her alone!"

"How the hell I'm gonna trust you?" asked the voice. "You can't give me no guarantees I can trust."

"I can sign something. Write whatever guarantee will satisfy you. I'll sign it!"

"That ain't gonna do it. You'll just tell your cop friends you signed under duress." After an interval, the voice said, "You got a camera?"

The colonel, somewhat less eagerly, said, "Yes, I have a digital camera. In my study. Next to the computer." A pause. "Why...what do you want it for?"

"I think I might got a way to keep you under control."

The world had become confused, a shadowy film blending lights and darks into a muddy constituency of unfamiliar objects. It seemed Aaron was dwindling, falling away inside the vastness of his own soul. With a mighty effort, he pushed against the presence that against all logic had invaded him. Less a push than an effort of will, of denial. After a brief struggle, the voice receded, reduced to a whisper, and the world was sharp again. He felt weak, tremulous, as though he had only just shaken off a delirium, but the sight of the fire lashing upward from the ember-coated logs served to steady him.

"Why do you want it?" the colonel repeated.

"I don't…" Aaron left the thought unfinished, still not quite certain of himself.

"Look, I don't know what you've got in mind. Whatever it is, I'm willing to listen. I'll go along…"

For no other reason than he wanted to stop the colonel from questioning him, Aaron hooked a log with the poker and dragged it out onto the floorboards. Blue flames danced up from the varnish.

"What are you doing?" The colonel stared at the log with horrified amazement, as though its presence abrogated a sacred principle.

"Stoking the fire," said Aaron, comfortable now with what he had done. "I'm quite cold."

He hooked a second log out to join the first, then plucked a burning stick of kindling from the hearth and proceeded about the room, torching the curtains one by one, while the colonel pled and cursed and screamed. The patch of floor in front of him was starting to catch, and flames from the curtains were licking at the ceiling. Before long the room was illuminated by a kind of hellish daylight, and the several fires came to have a greedy, lip-smacking sound. With a tremendous effort, the colonel succeeded in wriggling out of the chair and worm-crawled across the slick boards. The cords prevented him from making much progress. Dollops of burning pitch dripped from the edges of the ceiling, and one of the throw rugs caught and went to blazes in a matter of seconds, a little magic circle of heat and light. Smoke accumulated in the corners. The colonel propped his chin up on the boards, peered at Aaron, who stood not far from the entryway, and, each sentence more agonized than the one preceding, said, "What do you want? I'll do anything…anything you say. What do you want?"

A sprig of mercy brought forth a leaf in the wasteland of Aaron's emotions, but could not sustain growth amid the airlessness of the place. "Ask your questions of she who sent me. Ask them of Susan."

The colonel, with renewed desperation, wormed a few inches forward, then looked again to Aaron, words rushing out of him. "I'll tell you about Susan...everything I did to her. Just get me out!"

"You admit your guilt?"

Hesitantly, the colonel said, "Yes...yes! I'll tell you everything."

"Tell me quickly," said Aaron. "The fire is spreading."

Hope abandoned the colonel, and the residue of his strength dissolved. "Shoot me!" he implored. With his pleading eyes, his droopy mustaches, his checkered costume, he looked pitiable and clownish, an absurd figure trapped on stage during the first and final performance of an apocalyptic opera whose merry, crackling music was starting to outvoice its tenor's lament. Fringes of flame ate pitch from the seams of the boards above him; two leather chairs nearby began to smolder. He wriggled forward a few inches more. "For God's sake, shoot me! Don't leave me like this!"

As Aaron opened the door, the colonel spoke the last words he would utter to any worldly authority. "Come back!" he cried. "Christ! Come back!"

Aaron hurried down the path, not daring to stop and admire his handiwork, not wanting to stop. Every step he took, every impression of the dark watchful forest, every breath of cold, damp air, seemed each a more profound confirmation of the parasite that had attached itself to him, the black crablike creature-form of murder riding between his shoulders, infesting him, seeping into his flesh, until at length its every particle would converge inside his chest, there to counterfeit a heart. But as the fire came to roar at his back, to brighten the path ahead, he could not resist turning to watch the union of flames shape itself into a red-gold glove pointing skyward, exploding up from the enormous skull of pitch and logs it was consuming, as if to direct his attention to or announce his infamy to God. Embers showered upward from the conflagration, scattering onto the ground and among the boughs. The configurations of doors and windows showed demon black within garlands of yellow fire, and other structural features, too, seeming mystical in their design, were darkly visible within the blaze. This was the sight Susan had envisioned at her mad window, the vision she had employed him to create, yet he derived no joy from having pleased her. Sickness assailed him. Heart-sickness. His spirit tottered and lost balance on its platform of bone. He wandered off the path and sat upon one of the boulders that sprang from the moist, wormy earth, and without a thought of self-destruction, acting as if by reflex or upon instruction from some infinitely subtle source, he drew Colonel Rutherford's Colt and placed the barrel to his temple. One twitch, and the infirm essence that demanded immortality would be whisked away. It was unreal, the whole of it. The entire process a fabrication, every life a flimsy buttress of fear and violence contrived to shore up the rickety conventions of an insane narrative. No story truly ended. They were merely done with, slaughtered, left with broken necks and severed spines, starved, beaten, impaled, strangled, poisoned, eviscerated, axed, made ill, denied by justice, gutshot, blown up, drowned, and burned alive...eventualities which no reader mourned. Though it was plausible, he supposed, that such a story might be the product of a cosmic exercise in self-absorption, that it might have an author, a constellate figure whose mythic purpose it was to entertain an audience of one, a woman fashioned of stars and darkness, alone and unhappy in another quadrant of their lover's sky...

For reasons no more material than those that had moved him to suicide, though perhaps his appreciation of a universal indifference had some motive force, Aaron slipped the Colt into his pocket and set out along the path. It was much colder than it had been, a dampness that penetrated to the soul. He hunched his shoulders, wrapped his arms about himself, his thoughts leaping high and crackling with the dumb immediacy of flame, walking briskly as if he had somewhere to go and little time to get there.

✦

Rita found Dee at the end of the bar just as the band was calling it a night. They smooched, shared a dessert drink, smooched. Single men were wandering about, searching for their last chance; couples were leaving. The white stage lights brought up scars and scuff marks from the empty dance floor. The jukebox was on, but low. It was forty minutes to last call, and people were crowding the bar, trying to get drunk enough to drive. When Rita asked how it had gone with Janine, Dee made a woeful face. "I don't know. Maggie drove her home. I did the best I could for her."

"Well, if I'm a judge," said Rita with a grin, "that means she's probably feeling pretty good about now."

Dee blushed and spanked her on the arm. "Talking to Janine about anything serious, even when she's straight, she always makes it into a sarcastic game. She was going like..." Dee struck a pose and in an affected voice, said, "Like I totally understand. You're attracted to her.'" She gave a dismissive gesture. "After a while I just said, 'Fuck!' She'll probably call me tomorrow."

A bouncer pushed up to the bar beside them and spoke urgently to a chunky barmaid with dyed-black hair, grape lipstick, and a pierced nose. The barmaid reacted with a concerned look. Once the bouncer had left, Rita snared the barmaid's attention and asked what was wrong.

"Biker cut some guy in the parking lot," the barmaid said. "Gainer's useta be a biker hangout, and they hate the way the place is now. They come around all the time. I suppose they got nothing better to do than hassle people."

"It's a way of life for some," said Rita.

The barmaid turned liquor-service professional. "Can I get you ladies anything else?"

"Maybe couple shots." Rita looked to Dee, and then, together, they said brightly, "Tequila!"

"Two shots?" the barmaid asked.

"Better bring six," said Rita.

The barmaid pursed her lips. "You ladies driving?"

"I got a ride supposed to be coming," Rita told her. "He don't make it, we'll call a cab."

Dee acted disappointed. "You have a ride?"

"This friend of mine was gonna party with me tonight, but he had to finish a story. He might come by late to give me a ride home. I'm at a motel in Issaquah."

"He's a screenwriter?"

"Just stories."

Two guys in their thirties, salesmen maybe, with yuppie haircuts and mustaches, tried to move in, hemming them in against the bar, one saying, "I'm afraid of the dark—one of you ladies help me find my Ferrari?"and the other saying, "I told him to say that," and laughing, like it was a joke, like they'd been having a lame-line contest. Rita told them a ten-second story about the future and they left. Dee laid her head against Rita's, drew a kiss from the corner of her lips. "I want you to teach me everything," she said huskily.

"Only thing you need to know," said Rita, "is take what you want."

"I mean…" Dee hesitated. "About sex."

"I know what you mean. Sex is what I'm talking about. You take from someone, they take from you. If what you take is what they wanna give and vice versa, it's great. Sometimes it's great even if you don't fit that way."

Dee expressed confusion, and Rita said, "You telling me you don't know nothing about taking? You took from me tonight. Remember I wanted you to go slow? But you went right on and took what you wanted."

"I guess I didn't intend it that way." Dejection ground an edge off her good looks. "I thought you liked it."

"Aw, honey! I did! I gave you what you wanted. Give and take." She chucked Dee under the chin. "Next time I might want it hard and you give it slow. We'll work it out. We'll have us a night."

Another two-legged fly buzzed them, and this time Dee swatted it away.

"Take what you want." Rita lifted a second shot, peered at Dee through the tequila color. "It's the one rule you need to follow in life…especially you wanna be an actress."

A screw tightened behind Dee's gaze.

"That sound cold, does it?" Rita asked her.

"A little."

"That's 'cause it is. But it don't mean you have to ice up all through. You keep things separate. Cold's for the world. Hot's for your friends. Your true friends…and you ain't gonna have more than one or two of them."

"Are you going to be one of mine?"

Rita had a keen sense that the question was not altogether playful, that there was an undertone of hopefulness. She wasn't with Jimmy, she thought, she'd be tempted to say yes…even though Dee was trouble to the bone. "I can tell ya how it goes," she said. "I can tell ya how it all goes. I can show you how to make the decisions you'll need to if you're gonna be a taker. How to separate your mind from what you think you know and act on who you are." She did the shot, let the burn in her belly fade. "Years from now, that might make me a true friend. Your true friend. You might see it that way."

"But not now?"

"Things were different…maybe. But I'm on a whole different road from you. You know that."

Dee pressed her lips together and, with a forefinger, traced the letters spelling the name of the bar on a cocktail napkin.

Rita gave her a nudge. "Want me to tell ya how it goes?"

Dee built a solid nod from what started as little more than a tremor. "If you kiss me first."

"I can handle that," Rita said.

The kiss inspired her to do another shot, then a fourth. She was feeling it now. Drunk and ready to gamble. Looking at this grace of a girl with a fractured diamond soul who thought that she, Rita, was some kind of weird star, and maybe even saw through the disguise to the exact kind of star she was, an actress for real…it sparked her to think seriously about leaving Jimmy, about letting herself fall in love and dragging Dee off on as long and wild a ride as they could survive, mad nun and novitiate, arcing through heaven and burning out in the sky over Albuquerque or Minot or Coeur D'Alene. Waking up to that perfume-ad face on blue-mountain mornings north of Taos, or with gray mist and seabirds on San Juan Island. It might be worth the crack-up. Rita allowed the idea to get comfortable, to own her. Imagined they were already in that life. They sat on their stools facing in different directions, as on a love seat. She caressed Dee's waist, her thigh, kissing her, saying words that quickened her breath, and other words to teach her.

"Bad shit happens in life," she said. "Fucked-up love, rape, abuse…being poor. It's happened to me. Sometimes you can see who done it to ya, sometimes not. I've had people walk all over me, wipe their feet, spit, then just go on about their business. I couldn't even touch 'em."

"What did you do?" Dee whispered, and the whisper had a formal dimension, like the voice of a chorus issuing from beyond, a rapt prompting from the angels.

"What was I gonna do? I coulda wasted years goin' after 'em. There was times I did. But that just set me back. When somebody stops you from taking what you want, or takes something you don't wanna give, you keep it in mind, but y'don't let it control you. You just step to the side and go forward. It ain't easy, but you get the hang. And once you do, once you learn to use your frustration, your pain, there ain't a thing can stop you."

Dee said nothing, her breath fanning Rita's cheek.

Rita put some air between them so she could watch the girl, lost now in reflection. "You understand me. I know you do."

"I think…" Dee tilted her head, and her eyelids drooped. Then, animated, she said, "I think you want something from me." As if this had never happened before and she was happy to have something somebody wanted. The reaction made

Rita wary, made her wonder if she was sailing uncharted waters with this girl. And that gave her pause to wonder whether, really and for all, she could leave Jimmy. If this was something new, and something new didn't come along that often.

"Nothing you can't give," she said. "Nothing you don't want to give."

Dee embraced her so tightly, Rita wobbled atop the stool. "I'm going to fall in love with you tonight," Dee said, and Rita had an image of the words curving around her, like birds in flight carrying long streamers in their claws that they let fall about her shoulders, waist, and legs, settling light as crepe, encircling her, binding her beyond their apparent power. She felt the pressures of the girl's body specifically. Breasts, hips, arms, heart going like sixty. They would be crazy together, they would break rules she wasn't sure existed. She couldn't quite tell if she was buying into something, or if something had strolled past and snatched her up.

"Does that scare you?" Dee asked. "I'm scared."

"It ain't no good unless it's a little scary."

It seemed they were hanging, afloat on each other's warmth, the clutterish shouts and gabble and rattled glassware sounds of the bar forming a sky around them.

"Howdy," said a man's voice that Rita didn't recognize, but should have. She whipped her head around, ready to step on his tongue, and saw Jimmy standing there grinning in his suede jacket and stained cowboy hat. A moment's disaffection, wishing he was gone, seeing him dull and clumsy and unnecessary, and then she felt incredible relief, as if he was her hero and had hauled her back from the brink of a disaster. She pulled him in for a kiss and said, "Dee, this my friend Jimmy. The writer I told you about."

The two of them shook hands in a who-are-you-what's-this-gonna-mean-to-me way, and Jimmy said, "I know a guy named Dee over to Auburn."

Dee looked to Rita for support.

"Finish your story, Jimmy?" Rita asked.

"I think…mostly." He inserted himself between them and ordered a Coke from the barmaid, who was mixing a Tom Collins. "Probably do a little more on it come morning."

"Where'd you go tonight?"

He tipped back the brim of his hat, eyes narrowing with thought. "I don't know. I was just out driving. Trying to get things straight."

"This boy," Rita said to Dee, "he completely loses track. He goes off somewhere and zones out. Then he comes back with these beautiful stories. It's amazing!"

Dee, nervous, forced a smile. "Have you sold anything?" she asked Jimmy.

"Sold a few guns this weekend. Did all right by it. We gotta deliver a Colt up to Pullman in the morning."

"She means your stories, Jimmy," Rita said, beginning to wish once again that he hadn't shown up.

"They just something I do…stories. It ain't my business." He pointed at the Golden Bear emblem on Dee's T-shirt. "That's one fat ol' bear for him to be looking so fierce."

"Maybe we should leave," Rita said. "They about closed, anyway."

Jimmy said stubbornly, "I didn't get my Coke."

"Wouldn't be surprised you could get a Coke pretty much anywhere," Rita said. "Hey, I got an idea. Jimmy, whyn't you take my room at the motel? Then we can have time to talk over breakfast…or whenever we wake up. Me and Dee'll get a room's nice and fresh." Then, to Dee: "The maid service is just awful! They didn't clean me today or yesterday."

The lines of Jimmy's face had gone mulish and unhappy. Rita beamed a thought at him: Do not fuck this up for me.

"Yeah, okay." He dug two singles from his side pocket and tossed them on the bar.

As they headed for the exit, Jimmy in the lead, Dee took Rita aside. "Can we call a cab?" she asked, and Rita asked, "What's wrong?"

"I..." She nodded toward Jimmy, who had posted himself by the door and was waiting for them. "He seems so strange."

"I'm not strange?" Rita said. "You're not strange?" She threw an arm about Dee's shoulder. "He spaces when he's working. That's all it is."

A passing drunk jock with a teeny head atop massive shoulders and mesomorphic chest, his hair all sticking up and frosted yellow, said to Dee, "Golden Bears! Awright!" and she said, without turning, "Please die."

"How strange was that?" Rita said as he weaved off, knocking over a chair.

"I get your point." Dee slipped an arm around Rita's waist.

"Don't you worry. Can't nothing bad happen between you and me."

"You don't believe that," said Dee, like she knew.

Rita was already dressed when Jimmy came to pick her up the next afternoon. She answered his knock and slipped outside to talk with him, closing the door behind her. It looked as if he'd slept in his clothes. The day was gray and chilly, the lower sky graphed by electrical wires. Maybe a dozen crows were perched on a couple of the strands, like the notation of a boring melody. At the head of the alley that led to the rear of the motel, a man with a raggedy beard and carrying a half-full garbage bag, wearing a baseball cap and a down jacket patched with duct tape, was foraging in a dumpster. Rita felt stranded in the ordinary.

Jimmy jerked his head at the door. "She still here?"

"She's sleeping."

"Well, let's go."

A Greyhound bus wound out past the motel, interrupting them.

"We going to Pullman or what?" he asked gruffly.

"Yes, we're going! I just need to say goodbye. Unless you wanna go ahead on by yourself?"

"That what you want?"

"Quit being a dick! Warm up the goddamn van!"

She went back inside to warmth and the extraordinary, closed the door with a soft click. Dee was sleeping on her side; the sheet had slipped off her white shoulder. Rita sat beside her, stroked her hair until Dee made a lazy, contented sound, stretched, and fumbled for Rita's hand. She kissed the hand, then slid it down beneath the sheets, pressing Rita's fingers into the moist flesh between her legs. "See what you've done to me," she said muzzily.

"Time for me to go," Rita told her.

Dee scooted closer, laid her head in Rita's lap. "I know."

Rita had expected emotion, tears. "I'm talking about right now. Jimmy's out waiting in the van."

The girl rubbed her face languidly against Rita's belly, then, with effort, sat up, bracing on one hand. She pulled Rita into a hug and whispered, "We'll see one another again."

"You never can tell," Rita said. "But Berkeley's a long way from where I'm gonna be."

Dee shivered against her. "I can feel what's going to happen! Can't you feel it?"

"I'm feeling a lot of things, baby. I can't get 'em all straight just this minute."

Dee broke the embrace, gazed fiercely at her. "Why are you doing this?"

"I told you I was leaving."

"I don't mean that!" Dee flung off the covers, rolled out on the opposite side of the bed. She stalked to the door, kicked her T-shirt, which lay crumpled on the floor. She whirled about to face Rita, the cascade of her hair gracefully following a furious twist of her head. The pure lines of her body brought a thick feeling in Rita's throat.

"Why are you denying it!" Dee shouted. "How can you?"

The girl's anger seemed to flame out around Rita, as if she had stood too close when opening a furnace door. Its heat made her weak and uncertain. "I ain't denying nothing," she said.

"Liar!" Dee grabbed up the T-shirt, figured out where the arms were, and struggled into it, saying, "Liar!" again as she butted her head through the neckhole.

"You think I don't love you?" Rita came to her feet. "That ain't it. We wouldn't be no good together, honey."

She started toward the girl, but Dee stuck out a hand like a crossing guard restraining traffic, and said, "Don't touch me!"

"We'd have us a time," said Rita. "But we'd burn each other bad in the end. We both got a need to do that."

"You think you know *everything*," Dee said, becoming tearful.

"I may not..." Rita began, and Dee screamed, "Shut up! Shut up! Shut up!" and put her hands to her ears.

Rita stood mute. The puzzle of the girl, the moment, Jimmy outside, it flared in her, overwhelmed her; but then the brightness of emotion faded and she saw how to solve it. "You don't want me to touch you, you better give me room to pass," she said. "Otherwise I'll stand you aside."

Dee's anger sank to embers. She locked stares with Rita, then gave it up and took herself with quick steps to the far corner. She clasped her hands at her belly and watched Rita through the strands of hair barring her face with the intensity of an imprisoned saint.

Rita turned the doorknob, but didn't open the door. A hurt was brewing in her chest. "This how you want it?" she asked. "It ain't how I want it."

"Give and take," Dee said with steely precision. "Isn't that what this is?"

"If you say so, that's what it is."

Dee went on as if she hadn't heard. "All that shit you told me...that absolute shit!" She waved her hands in front of her face, a little mad girl frightened by a bee, and shrilled, "It was a line! Just like those fucks who hit on us at Gainers! Wasn't it?"

"It was and it wasn't," Rita said.

"Oh, don't go there! Don't you go there! Don't…don't…" Dee gulped in air or she might have hyperventilated. Gasping, she tried to speak, wheezed laughter instead. When she finally managed to say something, it was a scratchy whisper: "It is not. Everything is everything else. You're turning into Tony Roberts. Deepak Chopra. One of those assholes…"

"Try to calm down," said Rita, and opened the door a crack. "The things I told you, baby, they'll make sense down the road."

"I'm calm," said Dee, dragging hooked fingers through the tangles of her hair; then the rhythms of her speech grew rushed and histrionic. "I'm extremely fucking calm. You know why…you know why I'm so calm? Because I've figured it out. Actually that's not quite true. I've been *trying* to figure it out, but there wasn't anything *to* figure out, was there? You came right out and told us!" She parodied Rita's posture and voice. "'I'm an actress. I play the wise Indian woman who knows the secrets of the forest.'" She pointed an accusatory finger at Rita and her voice lowered in pitch. You were acting."

"You might wanna think about what acting really is," Rita said. "But yeah…you're halfway there."

"It was all a stupid fucking act!" Dee screamed, the effort taking her into a wild-haired crouch. "Wasn't it? Wasn't it?"

Rita nodded, less acknowledgment than a signing off. "I had a good night, baby. Best I had in years."

Dee ran forward as Rita passed through the door. "We'll see each other again," she said with resolution; and then, hurrying close as the door swept shut, her face the last thing Rita saw, she said despairingly, as if the message conveyed was a sad truth she had come to, "You don't know everything."

✦

The van, ugly and brown, quivered like an old bear as Rita climbed in. Inside, it had a mean burnt smell from the faulty heater, and she could smell, too, meanness smoking off of Jimmy. He didn't turn to her. Wedged beside his seat was the cedarwood box in which he'd packed the Colt. Rita had to slam her door twice to shut it.

They drove out onto the expressway without speaking. Jimmy took the van into the fast lane and made an angry game of driving, passing cars for no reason, then slowing down. He wanted to tell Rita something, but the thing he wanted to tell her was coiled up in his brain and wouldn't uncoil into a coherent sentence. He glanced over at her. She was resting her head against the window, watching the low hills stream past. "You look fucked out," he said.

Rita, who had been indulging in memories both sweet and bitter, rolled an eye toward him. "You always say just the right thing. Yes, I'm fucked out. Y'happy?"

Steamed, Jimmy whacked the steering wheel with his palm. "Yeah, I'm fucking delirious!"

The window glass shuddered against Rita's head. She felt heavy and feeble. The dead gray light ached in her eyes. "I told you when we started," she said wearily, "I was gonna fall in love every once in a while…and that's what happened. You got no cause to be all pissy."

"'Pissy'," he said, trying out the word for its fit. "I ain't 'pissy.' What I am is fed up."

"It's a constant source of pain to ya, is it?"

He shot her another glance, fuming mad.

Rita closed her eyes, saw hot pinlights behind the lids. "When's the last time this happened, Jimmy?"

"A year…" he started, and then he thought about it and couldn't remember. "Don't matter when. I'm still sick of it."

"Almost two years ago. Tacoma."

"All right," he said. "So?"

"So—" Rita sat up, getting her ginger back "—if I go off the tracks every couple years and get right back on like I always do, I don't see it being such a sore point with you. Especially since I give you fair warning."

He saw the right of this, but wasn't ready to relinquish anger. "A man's got pride in hisself, he doesn't like to see his woman goin' off with anyone. But fallin' in love with another woman...That ain't goin' off the tracks, that's goin' off the edge of the goddamn Grand Canyon!"

"Fuck you!" Rita squirmed around so she was almost sideways in her seat. "I don't wanna hear any shit about what a man's got. Like you some kinda unique creation I can't understand. I hate that shit!"

"All right. Fine. *I* got pride! *I* don't wanna see my woman runnin' off with somebody else!"

"Then you best look away when the occasion arises," she said. "Just like I do when you start fooling around with the Loretta Snows of the world."

The thought of Ms. Snow tangled Jimmy in a confused memory, and he lost track of being angry. He backed off the gas and drove along in the smoky wake of a furniture van, which was laboring up the first dark green step of the Cascades.

"That man-woman rules-for-living bullshit ain't about us," Rita said a while later. "You know that, Jimmy. We got our own thing."

"I'm still a man," he said. "You still a woman. No way you can eliminate the fact."

"Don't get simple on me. Y'know what I'm talking about."

He drove for a half mile without saying anything, then asked, "What was she screeching for back there?"

"I was advising her about life," said Rita.

"She sure was acting crazy."

"I don't believe she was acting. But you never know."

"What kind of advice you give her? Musta been pretty fucking heavy."

"Jesus, Jimmy! What do you care?" She tapped his leg. "Pull over! I wanna drive."

"I'm okay," he said. "I'll let you know when I'm tired."
"Come on. Pull over!" she said. "I'll drive and you can tell me the end of your story."

The story took them through the Cascades and down into the rolling brown hills of the Palouse. Traffic was almost nonexistent and as Jimmy talked, Rita let the van drift over the center line when the wind buffeted it, swerving to avoid the tumbleweeds that rolled like bewitched nests across the two-lane road. The sky had opened up to the north, a gunmetal-blue streak ledging the horizon, and clouds raced low above them, their bellies swollen dark, hurrying to join the greater darkness gathering over the mountains they had left behind. They passed through cuts with yellow walls of packed earth tufted by sage and emerged onto vistas from which they could see more hills, more tumbleweeds, more brown and yellow, the highway winding and humping off toward the edge of the world like a dirty white rope dropped by a giant fleeing the apocalypse that had stripped all but a spark of life from the land.

As Jimmy wound it down, Rita wondered how much he knew of what of he'd done, or, for that matter, how much she knew. She had a pretty good idea, but there was a world of difference between knowing and knowing for sure. His stories troubled her as much as they stirred her, because while she could nudge them this way and that, in the end he was the one who controlled the situation, both their own and that of the story. Being swept along with him, the risk of it, worried that he might make a bad mistake, it was exhilarating, it was what she wanted; but she wished she knew for sure what he had done so she could sweep up his mess if need be. She watched him out of the corner of her eye, the long, formal sentences spooling forth, telling the doom of Colonel Rutherford. With his dull exterior and the incomprehensible machinery inside, he was like, she thought, a bomb that shined a beautiful light when it exploded, then reassembled itself, ready to go again when the right command was given.

"Didn't come out good as I wanted," he said after he had done. "It's like I had something else in mind, and it didn't get done."

"You always feel like that," Rita said. "And don't I always tell ya, you turn out the best damn stories I ever heard? This one turned out extra good."

"Yeah, but it don't make sense to the way I thought it was going."

"Which way's that?"

He thumped the latch of the glove compartment, trying to piece together the unrealized parts of the story.

"Reach in there and see if there's a candy bar," Rita told him.

He rummaged about, found nothing edible. "Okay," he said. "I was planning to have Susan recognize that she loved Aaron, too, and they'd consummate their love, 'cause forbidden though it was, there was something pure about it, something they couldn't find with nobody else. That'd give her the strength to leave the colonel." He closed the glove compartment, said, "I'm not sure what was gonna happen after that."

"I like how you told it better," Rita said. "You leave the colonel alive, he'd take his temper out on Susan's daddy."

"Her daddy wasn't important…wasn't hardly in the story. And the colonel, a man like that, somebody's gonna get around to killing him sooner or later. Thing I wanted was for Susan to leave him without getting more screwed up'n she was."

"Maybe she heard an inner voice told her not to do ol' Aaron."

A note of satisfaction in the words grated on him. "Hell you so happy about? I screw up my story and it makes you happy?" The glove compartment door fell open and banged his knee; he jammed it shut. "Inner voice…shit!"

"Women get voices telling them things. Female intuitions. Susan come to life on ya is what happened."

"Saying women hear voices, that's like me saying a man's got his pride."

"No," said Rita. "It ain't the same thing at all."

Jimmy's head lolled against the window, and she thought he had gone to sleep, but then she heard him muttering, whispering, maybe off on some loop of the story that hadn't quite finished with him. Or thinking ahead to another story that had yet to find its .45 caliber inspiration. The wind blew stronger, steadier, and she had to fight for the road, especially at the tops of the hills. From one of those heights she observed a herd of tumbleweeds stampeding over a wide brown and yellow plain, hundreds of them, aiming for the highway about half a mile farther along. Dried-up yellowish gray wheels, some as big as semi tires. When they hit the margin of the pavement, a few hopped high, like frightened kangaroos; the rest kept up their dervish pace, traveling west by north into the Devil's country. Signs everywhere, she thought. She was back in Browning, she might run to see Mrs. Buffalo Knife and ask what they meant. But she didn't need a wise woman to read them now. They all told the same meager, miserable thing about life.

Jimmy's muttering grew louder, and then he said something in an odd lilting delivery.

"What's all that?" Rita asked.

He blinked at her and said, "'One man's gun shot out the sun.'"

"Yeah, that's what you said. What is it?"

He took to repeating the line with varying emphasis until Rita grew irritated.

"The first time," she said, "it was like you sang it kinda."

He tried singing the words, softly, hoarsely, then said, "Guess that's all I can do for now. But I believe we got us another one coming."

They came up over a rise, and directly ahead, lying in the middle of the road, was an open suitcase with someone's clothes still in it, the sleeves of a sweater flapping emptily, looking as if a magician's assistant who had been made invisible was now being drawn down inexorably into his master's bag of tricks. Rita had to cut the tires hard to avoid it.

"I don't know," said Jimmy, tired now, and indifferent to the world. "Maybe it'll be a song."